The Way In

Also by Eugene Mirabelli / **The Burning Air**

The Way In

a novel by

Eugene Mirabelli

New York / The Viking Press

For **Margaret Anne**

The Way In

1

I, Frank Annunzio, tell you this story. Some years ago—I was twenty-two at the time—I quit my job, packed my clothes into a suitcase, and set out in search of my future.

Often before then some urge had almost sent me off, but I had always felt unprepared and had never gone. Besides, I suspected the urge was immoral. Most men, powerful and respected men, were happy to trade away the best part of their lives for money, content to work out the destinies of others. It seemed I was the only one who wanted to keep his own life in his own hands. Once I even went around asking people were they ever nudged by these same impulses and they said, "No. Not at all," or else they laughed and slapped me on the shoulder, saying, "Yes. I was young once too." Those answers always made me uneasy. Ever since I could remember, I had felt different from other people, yet I always had a longing to be like everyone else. Now, outside I looked all right but inside I was still somewhat crazy. Because down inside me the inner man was no longer just knocking at my heart, he was kicking around, struggling to take over. Let me take back what I said earlier: I did not set out in search of my future. This inner man did not give a damn about my future and when at last I quit my job it was like jumping off the roof or falling into bed with the most desirable wrong woman but it was not what you would call looking for a future. I am trying to tell you the truth. Everyone seemed to have taken care of his soul quite neatly except me. I never learned how they handled this because no one ever told me and I gathered that it would have been indelicate to ask. It seemed their souls were white, folded, and pressed flat, then tucked away so deftly that only the edge showed. I did not know the color of my soul but I guessed it was all wadded up, crumpled into a ball, and jammed away somewhere. Still, I hoped it was bigger than a handkerchief. I wanted to unravel it, unfold it, spread it out broader than a bed sheet or a table cloth. I wanted it to tower tall and wide, stretched out like the sails on a clipper ship.

Then there was this young woman named Alba. Our affair had been on again, off again, for two years and now I asked her to marry me. During the summer her parents rented a small cottage on Cape Cod on the dunes overlooking the sea, but no one was living in it except Alba and her roommate from college days, and the roommate usually went away to a boy friend's place when I came down. We had the cottage all to ourselves that weekend. We talked a lot. When the sun was too hot for us we went in swimming, and at night there was a cool breeze and we tried to make love, but mostly we just talked. By Sunday afternoon we had said all we ever had to say. We were finished.

The ferry which was going to take me back to Boston was to leave in a little while, so we walked into town and down to the harbor together. The sun was bright. Alba was wearing white shorts and a white jersey and was barefoot, but I was in my city clothes. I felt hot and overdressed and out of place. The square was filled with people in sport shirts, slacks, shorts, sun dresses, tennis shoes, sandals, bathing suits. We went along the shaded edge of the square and walked out onto the long wharf. The ferry was sided with some sort of bright metal clapboard which dazzled in the sun. I went over to the ticket booth and bought my passage, then we walked back along the wharf. When we reached the square I stopped at a stand to buy a magazine.

"Buy me something?" Alba asked.

"Yes. Sure. What do you want?"

"A pair of sunglasses."

There was a rack of low-priced sunglasses on the counter. Alba tried on a pair, took them off, tried on another, took them off, and began looking at some others.

"They all look pretty cheap to me," I said. "Why don't we go someplace else and get you a good pair?"

"No. These are all right." She snatched up another pair, then tore them off. "Here. These are excellent."

I paid for the sunglasses and gave them back to Alba. She did not wear them but kept twisting them by the stem while we looked around for some place to go. The sun was hot. At the corner of the square by the pier was a restaurant with a small terrace built out over the water; it had a few round metal tables and a white canvas awning for shade, so we went there. We were the only ones. We drank iced coffee and looked at the wide bay without saying anything. Some darkly tanned boys in bathing suits were running along the edge of the wharf, shouting at a group of people going to the ferry. The group paused—the boys took up diving positions —someone tossed a coin over the water and the boys sailed after it, dropping through the air and plunging into the sea. We finished the iced coffee and now people were strolling down the wharf to the ferry. I looked across at Alba and found her watching me.

"Did I give you the key?" I asked her. "Are you going to be able to get back in?"

"Yes. I have it. Everything is all right. Yes."

"What time are your parents arriving?"

"Sometime tonight. I don't know exactly when."

The ferry horn sounded. I called the waitress over and paid for our iced coffee. When I turned back to Alba she had put on the sunglasses; they gave her a blind, blank look. I picked up my overnight suitcase and Alba grabbed my raincoat. We crossed over to the wharf and hurried toward the ferry. A boy shot past us, dove off the edge of the wharf, and began swimming to the others who were already treading water by the ship and shouting up at the passengers. When we reached the gangway we stopped and I turned to Alba. I could not make out her eyes behind the black sunglasses.

"Why not come down next weekend?" she asked. "My mother won't bother us. You can sleep out on the porch."

"Or maybe you can come to me. Take the ferry some afternoon. You can stay at my place overnight. You can even sleep in my bed."

The black glasses glittered, her face went stiff and dead. She thrust the raincoat into my arms and backed away a step. Someone ran past us up the gangway.

"For God's sake," I said. "Take off those damned sunglasses."

She tore them off and gave me a blazing look. Her eyes were glistening on the verge of tears.

"I love you," I said. "Do you know that?"

She put her hand to her mouth and ground the knuckles into her teeth and looked at my eyes. I moved to touch her, but her fist shot out and smashed me in the chest. And that was the end of that.

2

Now five years later I walked up the gangway and boarded the same ship. The engines had begun to throb, the horn boomed and boomed, the town gave back an echo. The ship was named *The Voyager:* a long square hulk with glittery chromium flanks, peeling and freckled with rust. During the summer it left Boston at ten each morning and sailed to Provincetown, then after a stopover it sailed back and reached Boston near eight in the evening. I checked my suitcase and raincoat in the baggage room, took a turn around the deck, then leaned on the aft rail and watched the land go down. The wharf had already sunk to a splinter and the piles had turned to pins. The waterfront buildings looked flat and now they were squeezing back against each other, shrinking little by little until they were a cluster of colored marks standing over a flooded harbor. Above the town there was a low green hill, dotted here and there with houses and surmounted by the Pilgrim Tower. After a while the hill was hazy and the town was blurred and the land seemed a flat gray shadow on the horizon.

Cape Cod begins some miles south of Boston where an arm of the shore reaches eastward into the Atlantic and swings slowly upward to the north; Boston stands as its head, Provincetown is tucked in its palm. When Columbus sailed from Spain he headed due west, and if God had seen fit to keep his ships on course he would have run aground on the Cape, for it lay directly in his path. From a distance it looms across the water like an endless golden shore overhung with green meadows and hazy blue hills. On windless nights the air is sweet with the odor of bayberry and pine, and in the morning everything lies in a milky blue mist. When you wade ashore all this vanishes. The green fields melt into swamps of eel grass, the bright earth melts into slime; further inland the meadows are brown, covered with brittle grass and bordered with stunted oak, scrub pine, and thorny locust trees. Here and there the dirt is cracked, revealing the sand which lies beneath it all. Bradford and his Pilgrims aimed to sail southwest across the Atlantic to Virginia, but God raised certain winds and blew them way around Race Point and into the smooth gray waters of Cape Cod Bay. They coasted along the silent beaches, went ashore now and again, then settled finally on one rocky patch and set about to create New England out of the void.

Toward evening we sighted the islands which lie near the port of Boston. They appeared misty gray, then became brown-and-dun-colored rocks capped with bright green grass. One of the islands was built up into a small fortress; there was grass growing in the cracks between the stone blocks and on top were some ancient cannon aimed out to sea. We passed a bell buoy which plunged and swayed majestically in our wake, clanging. Then the city grew up on the horizon, low and gray with some towers here and there and spires and a dome. The sun was setting and the sky above the city was light green, and then beyond the buildings there was gold. The passengers began to gather their belongings; I went to the baggage room, picked up my suitcase and raincoat, and returned to the deck. We glided gently through the dark water at dockside. The ship crushed slowly against something, jostling us, then it shook and ceased and we had landed.

I went down into the subway and headed homeward. In the North End, the Italian part of Boston, a festival was going on. People were strolling around, there was band music, and the air was blazing with lights—trellises, arches, ropes of light. The buildings were draped with red, white, and green bunting and at the far end of this tunnel of hot white bulbs there was a colorful church façade. I made my way through the crowds along the sidewalk until I came to a restaurant, then went in and ate my supper. When I came out the sidewalks were overflowing and people were walking in the street. I started drifting down toward the band music. A banner sagging above the street said: GRANDE FESTIVITÁ RELIGIOSA DI S. ANTONIO DI PADOVA. Along the curb pushcarts were selling *torrone* candy, fake jewelry, rosary beads, and there were booths with pizza, ice cream, coffee, soda, boiled corn, and statues of the Virgin Mary. The musicians were seated on folding chairs at the foot of the dazzling church front. I bought a mug of coffee and listened to them play. Actually there were two bands which took turns: the Napoli Band on the left played marches, the Roma Band on the right played opera. The two conductors were spirited but the bands played badly and no one was listening anyway. People were strolling up and down and milling about, looking for pickups, standing in bunches with their arms folded, scratching their elbows, talking, laughing. I found some good-looking strays here and there, but they eyed me once and then went blank. I was really out of it with my raincoat on my arm, my little suitcase. Everyone looked vaguely familiar, but the Italian always seemed to be in a dialect I could not catch. The church face was made of wood nailed to a scaffolding about three stories tall. A big round window had been sawed from the center and filled with a starry pattern of colored paper. The rest of the surface was illuminated with enamel paint and inlaid with silver and gold foil. It looked cheerful. On the corner of Prince Street there was a movable grotto, like a sentry box, and standing inside it was a life-size statue of S. Antonio of Padua. I finished my coffee and went over to look. Saint Anthony was dressed in a loose brown cassock—it was real cloth put over the statue—with a rope around his waist, and in his right hand he carried an open book. The child Jesus balanced on the book, holding Saint Anthony's shoulder and blessing us, or maybe just waving. The Saint's robe glittered with rows of pocket watches and gold rings, and from the walls of his cell hung long ribbons fringed with crisp-looking paper money. I wondered what Saint Anthony's regalia was all about. He was my patron saint but I knew almost nothing about him. People were shoving around to get a close look at the statue and to add up the money, so I moved out of the way. I boarded the subway again. The cars rattled up from underground, swayed gently over the black waters of the Charles River, then slanted down into Cambridge and roared along, emptying at last beneath Harvard Square. Now I had only a short walk home.

3

Before I go on with this story let me say that I am thirty-two years old. I was conceived on a rainy afternoon in a hotel room in Florence, during the last week of December, while my parents were on their wedding trip. They had been sightseeing, and in the Piazza della Signoria my mother had stopped at the foot of the naked statute of David and said to my father, "I want to have a boy like that." My mother first told me this story when I was rather young, and made me proud of myself; several years passed before I realized that she was really honoring my father. I was born on the fourth of October in Boston, Massachusetts. I suppose that when I was a baby I discovered my own flesh, discovered that I was living inside a body, but I must have gone on to other things soon after because I have no memory about it. As far as I remember, the first time I actually saw myself I was seven years old. That summer my parents took me to the beach, and each day when the tide was out I used to play in the shallow water between the sand bars and try to catch the minnows as they swam between my ankles. One afternoon I found that the ends of my fingers had become pale and wrinkled from so much water, and when I looked closely I saw that my fingers and palms were patterned, lined with a swirl of little ridges. I touched the fingertips of my left hand to the fingertips of my right so the ridges seemed to interlock, and when I pressed my palms together I saw the marvelous symmetry of my hands, then of my whole body, and suddenly I recognized that my left side was a mirror of my right. My mother and father were sitting side by side on the shore, and as I walked back to them I saw where the waves had left the sand bars all rippled and whorled, like giant fingerprints, and it came to me that my symmetry was born from my parents—my mother had given me my left side, my father had given my right—and God had put the two halves together.

I guess that whenever I thought about it I understood that I was born in my mother, knew that I kicked awhile inside her before arriving here, but I never knew, never even wondered what all this might mean to her. And certainly it was not a thing that she would ever talk about. Only once she came close to it, when she was coming up dazed from an anesthetic. My father was sitting on a chair beside her hospital bed and he said she was asleep. I asked him how she was going to be. "Fine," he said. "But they were afraid it might go bad and cause trouble later. So they took everything out." My mother opened her eyes and looked around until she found us, then she closed her eyes. "I'm still a woman," she murmured. "I'm too old to start growing a beard. I've had three children. You can't be a mother unless you're a woman—" And she began to weep softly. My father stood up, looked at me, then sat down and took her hand. He told her everything was going to be all right. Mother opened her eyes to look at him, then closed them and said, "They can't turn me into the Virgin Mary." Then she went back to sleep. A year after my mother recovered from the hysterectomy my father had his prostate cut up. I had been away and he did not know I was coming to visit him, but when I reached his room the door was ajar enough for me to enter. My father was getting out from the far side of the bed, with his back to me, and he was wearing one of those loose white shirts that tie together with strings in the back. As he sat up the shirt fell open and I saw his thin yellow shoulders and withered behind—he pitched forward, grabbed the bedpost, shuddered, and sat still for a long time. I waited in the doorway while he eased himself off the bed and slowly reached for his robe, then I stepped back into the hall and stood there until I heard him shuffling about. Then I knocked loudly and went in. He was seated in a chair but he was still trembling. I lighted a cigar for him and he sat by the window and talked. Father's hands looked just like mine, but much older, and after we said good-by I kept looking at my hands and thinking how whatever made me a man came from him, came right out of him.

A couple of years ago I saw some of my own sperm, peered at them through a microscope. At first it was like looking at a dish full of wheat grains, or rice, while you shake the dish and everything jiggles around and about. When I increased the power of the microscope, focused it again, it was like looking onto a stadium full of wild football players. It was a sad and angelic sight to watch: those lost fragments of myself kept racing around, going on and on, trying to find the one other half that would make them whole.

On Monday morning I signed the lease on my apartment for one more year, chopped up my paintings, and strolled over to Research/Research. The sun was high and the air was damp, warm. R and R was on Brattle Street in a wooden house which had been built around 1830: shingle roof, white clapboards, and windows that went from the ceiling to the floor. It had been someone's home up to a few years ago; then an architect bought it, cleaned the insides, set up an office for himself on the left, and rented three rooms on the right to Research/Research. Marian Malone, our secretary, was reading a book and drinking coffee when I walked in and said, "Hello, Marian, how's life?"

She lowered her book slightly and looked at me. "Hello, lover." Marian was thirty-something years old and unmarried.

I asked her if Scott was in.

"He's in but he's on his way out. Are you coming back to work?"

"Yes. Is Scott busy right now?"

"He's dictating letters into the machine. For me to type. He wants to make sure I'm not bored while he's away. How long are you back for this time?"

I said I did not know how long and asked when could I see him. She buzzed his telephone, told him I was here, and told me he would be out in a minute. "Want some coffee?" she asked.

While we drank coffee I told her about my vacation and she told me about Ibera, the architect across the hall. He was secretly looking for a new secretary. Scandinavian design was in fashion with his school of architecture and Ibera wanted a Scandinavian secretary to greet his clients. The past couple of years he had employed girls with lovely Swedish accents but each one had left to get married; Marian had attended the weddings of the last two. Now he was using an American blond with a Swedish name, a girl who thought she knew everything about everything, and Marian did not get along with her. The door to the inner office had opened and Scott was advancing on me. He was a big man, the biggest I have ever known. His face was square and red, his hair shaggy white. He looked quite jovial.

"So," he said. "There you are." His handshake was always delicate, shy.

"Yes. Here I am."

"I'll have my secretary put you on the payroll." He turned, shifted his weight toward Marian. "Put Mr Annunzio on the payroll."

"Sure thing," Marian said. She gathered up our coffee cups and went down the hall to wash them out.

"How was your vacation?" he asked.

"It was a vacation."

He studied me a moment. "How have you been?"

"I've been all right, actually. And you?"

"I'm living." Now he looked gloomy.

"Marian tells me you're going on a trip."

"Yes," he said vaguely. "Down to Washington, then over to California, then back to Washington. And then back up here. A rotten schedule." He was melancholy, all right.

"How's the business?"

"We meet our expenses. We keep moving." He paused, speculating. "Come and have lunch," he said abruptly.

"I just finished breakfast."

"Come along anyway," he said, moving into his office. "Just up the street. The Empress J." He came out, pulled the door shut, and locked it.

I told him I was not hungry and that I didn't have a necktie on.

Marian had come in with the washed coffee cups. Scott told her that he and Mr Annunzio were going out for lunch now and should be back in an hour or less. He guided us toward the front door. "He leaves for Washington at one-thirty," Marian called out after me.

The Empress J was a neat gray clapboard house turned into a French restaurant; the interior had been scrubbed and repapered, but the walls were still in place so you had to sit at little Empire tables in somebody's former dining room or living room or drawing room. These domestic chambers made me feel like an intruder, but Scott had developed a taste for French cooking a few years ago in Paris, and now he enjoyed eating here. He lowered himself tentatively onto the chair, and when it did not collapse he relaxed. He scanned the handwritten menu. "Let's celebrate," he said. "What are you going to have?"

"Nothing," I said. "I'm not hungry."

"Nothing?" He looked baffled, then hurt.

"Nothing at all."

Scott's doctors had told him he was eating too much and had put him on a diet; when he ate alone he kept to the diet but when he dined with anyone he turned the meal into a feast, a banquet. A waitress came and asked if we would like something to drink. I said I did not want anything, Scott said he wanted a martini. The waitress left and we sat in silence a long time. He looked very morose.

"I would like to die on a full stomach," he said.

Scott had high blood pressure and gout and a few years ago he had been laid out with hepatitis. The waitress brought the martini and asked if we would like to order now. Scott looked at his plate and did not say anything. Finally I ordered two omelets and Scott quickly added that he wanted his omelet laced with cheese and garnished with mushrooms and I don't remember what all else. He was benign now. I asked him why he was going to Washington.

"Conference at the Pentagon."

"What do they want?"

"They want to know how to talk to the enemy."

"Sounds interesting," I said.

I was not interested. He said the Pentagon had decided that it was sometimes the best strategy to keep enemy forces informed on the power and location of our own forces. He spoke for a long while in bits and pieces about the report he was taking to the Defense Department conference, then went on to talk about one of the contracts he hoped to bring back from California. He was going to spend a few days in Los Angeles, then a few in San Francisco. He was dispirited about spending the weekend in some San Francisco hotel, I forget which one.

"Maybe you'll have time to visit your daughters," I suggested. Two married daughters lived in San Francisco.

"I wrote to them," he said crisply. "They know my routes. They know my timetable."

I did not say anything. He had told me before about his daughters and how they were beautiful and ungrateful and wasted.

"I'll telephone them when I get there," he said abruptly. "They will have decided by then whose turn it is to endure me for what.

One husband will meet me at the hotel and take me home to dinner. After dinner we will all drive over to the other house for dessert and small talk. Very small talk. Then the other husband will drive me back to the hotel. That way everyone suffers just a little bit."

"How's Heather?" Heather was the third and youngest child, a college student, his favorite.

"She's still working in New York. I assume. At least that's what she wrote to her sisters at the beginning of the summer vacation."

After that we talked about nothing until the end of lunch. Scott paid the waitress and while we were waiting for her to return with the change he said it was good to have me back. Then he asked how long was I planning to work for him.

"About a year," I said. "Off and on."

"You don't know?"

"Call it a year."

The waitress brought back the change in a little wooden tray, blue with gold fleurs-de-lis.

"Well," Scott said. "I have a great admiration for painters." He added some change to the pieces in the tray. "My father was a painter, you know."

"Yes. You told me."

"He never grew wealthy."

"But he made a living at it." I knew the story.

"Yes, he made a living at it. A portrait painter can make a lot of money if he's fashionable. He gets to be a favorite of the rich, then they all want to have their portraits painted by him. But my father was never fashionable. He had his own style. Everyone wanted a portrait by Sargent or something that looked as if it had been painted by Sargent. But my father had his own style and he never tried to please the rich. He told me once that all he really had was his style and that he would put away his brushes before he would paint like anyone else." He paused, remembering. "He was trying to explain why we were poor. He hated being poor."

I didn't know what to say. "I looked him up in Fielding's *Dictionary*. He won some prizes. He must have been all right."

"He was a good father," he said distantly.

When we got back to the office Marian was typing rapidly. A loose-leaf folder lay open on her desk beside a neat stack of clean typed pages. She looked very efficient. "Your wife phoned just after you left," she told Scott. "She should be here just about now to drive you to the airport." She went back to typing.

Scott unlocked the door to the inner office and called me after him. He opened the safe beside his desk, took out two notebooks, and gave them to me. "Edit these. It will keep you busy while I'm away," he added.

I asked if there was anything else he wanted me to do.

"Have a chair. Relax." He lowered himself gently into his swivel chair.

I sat down. Scott turned and studied the blackboard on which he had chalked a few names and places and some abbreviated sentences. He had a good office. The walls were pale, almost white, and in the back two large windows looked onto a lawn with a gravel walk and a crabapple tree. A wooden bench encircled the trunk of the tree, and it must have been pleasant long ago to sit down there and talk, or to lie alone on the grass, looking up into the leaves. The glass in the window and the door was bordered with a thin strip of silvery metal; it was part of the alarm system. The typing had ceased. Now we heard Marian and Mrs Scott talking in the next room. Scott rose and wearily erased the blackboard. He picked up his brief case and I handed him that huge raincoat. We went to the outer office.

"These are your plane tickets." Marian picked up two little folders and gave them to Scott one at a time. "And this is your schedule of appointments."

"Hello, Frank." Mrs Scott was a rather tall woman with neat gray hair. She was wearing a tan summer suit.

"Hello, Alice," I said. She always told me to call her by her first name. She watched me a moment, then smiled briefly. "What have you been doing?" she asked me.

"A little of everything."

She turned to her husband. "Have you forgotten anything?"

"Let's go," he said.

Marian went on with her typing. The car was parked beneath the side window, a black Mercedes crusted with mud. Mrs Scott took the wheel and started the motor while her husband eased himself in beside her. The car crunched slowly backward over the gravel drive into the street, then it turned and slid away.

"You can stop typing now."

Marian dropped her hands into her lap, sighed. "You never can tell. She might take a look in on her way back from the airport."

I asked her did she want to go out to get herself lunch; she said no, she had brought an egg-salad sandwich from home. After the sandwich she had a cup of black coffee. I said something about her not eating much.

"I'm on a diet," she answered. "For all the good it does me."

"You have a splendid figure, Marian. You're just not my type, that's all." She was a sturdy woman, with a massive face and bushy black hair.

"I'm not anybody's type, that's all."

"How's Kevin these days?" She was more or less engaged to this Kevin O'Connell.

"Who knows?" She started to say something, then stopped. "He's very busy getting ready to teach. School opens in a couple of weeks."

She folded her sandwich paper into a small neat square and dropped it into the wastebasket. I had never met Kevin, but from what Marian had told me during the past year I knew that the two had their ups and downs. We talked a while longer, then Marian set aside her cup and arranged her desk. She laid out her folders and some clean typed pages, put a fresh sheet in the typewriter, and typed half a dozen lines. Then she took out her novel and went back to reading. I went into my office and spread one of the note-books Scott had handed me: the first report was a survey of research on a fish, the *Gymnarchus niloticus*. I told Marian I would see her next morning, and went out for a long walk.

4

Later that afternoon I telephoned Helen Shawn at her office and asked her was she doing anything that evening. "Absolutely nothing," she said. "Come to dinner." Helen Shawn was Alba's roommate, the roommate who used to go out whenever I came down to spend a weekend with Alba on the Cape. One freezing day on Boston Common we recognized each other, stopped to exchange hellos, and I asked her to have a cup of coffee. In the cafeteria she asked what I had been doing since last summer. I had been doing nothing much but now I was going off to teach in a private school. "It's in the woods, and I was just taking a last look at the city. And you?"

"Secretary," she said.

"You're not married."

"No. I'm not married and I'm not engaged to be married. You had heard?"

"I had heard you were going to be."

"I thought I was pregnant, that's all. He said he would marry me if I got an abortion first, but if I had the baby he would run out. He said he would get ten of his friends to say they might be the father, something like that. It turned out I was all right so I sent him his ring back."

She told me his name and asked if I had ever met him. I had never heard of him.

"A real rat," she said. "Afterward he told all his friends I was a whore and sent them around to visit me."

I said something inane about some people being bad for each other. "Alba and I always wound up—"

"No. No. Please." She smiled gently and pressed her finger tips to her ears as if to blot out the sound of my voice. "I don't want to know about anything. At least not about your girls."

I would have said I didn't have so many girls, but she did not want to hear anything more on that from me. We talked a bit longer, then I had to leave to catch a train. She took a tiny red leather notebook from her purse, tore out a page, and wrote her address. "I live in Cambridge with three other girls," she said. "Come visit us when you get back to civilization."

Now she lived alone, a ways up Massachusetts Avenue in a four-story building, under the roof. It was a tiny apartment: a narrow room with the kitchenware at one end and two windows over the avenue at the other end—she had some bright thin scatter rugs, a couple of lawn chairs, a bookcase made of loose bricks and boards holding rows of paperback novels and college texts on political science—the bathroom was in a closet and the bedroom in an alcove off the living room. It was hot in there and Helen was slicing up a salad. "Make yourself a drink," she said, turning away. "Dinner is almost ready."

I opened the wooden packing box where she kept her alcohol. "What would you like?" I asked. Inside were three square gin bottles, a sherry, a good scotch, an empty bourbon, and an unopened brandy.

"Whatever you're having."

"I'm having a sherry."

"Pour me a scotch on ice."

I made the drinks, set the scotch on ice on the counter by the salad, and went over to the open windows. She had arranged a couple of chairs around the coffee table made from an inlaid chess board; I sat in the wicker chair because it looked cool, but there was no breeze and it was hot. Helen came over with her drink and sat opposite me. She shut her eyes and very slowly drew a long strand of damp hair back from her cheek. I had known her too long to think about her features, but other men said she was attractive. She looked at me, smiled.

"How are you, Helen?"

"Quite bored. But you're back and that's good."

I agreed that I was back.

"On the same job as before?"

"Yes."

"Well, I'm glad you came back." She started to smile. "Even if your work is lewd and obscene, I'm glad you came back."

"Thank you."

"Now tell me what you did. Where did you go? Who did you see?"

"I visited friends, mostly. Maine. Connecticut. New York. And then to the Cape, alone." We talked a while about places in Maine, some friends in New Hampshire, a play in New York. She asked about the Cobbles; Helen had met the Cobbles only once, but ever since then she liked to hear about them. I told her about my weekend at their wild farm. She asked how many children they had now; four, I told her.

"That's how many they had last time," she said. "I thought they'd have more by now."

"Laura runs the house so it looks like they have six. Let that console you."

"I like her." She sipped her drink and gazed musingly out the window. "Did you happen to see the Benjamins in your travels?" The Benjamins were friends of ours who used to live in Cambridge.

"I saw Ben. I didn't see Jane. They just got a divorce."
She looked at me, startled. "What happened?"

"He went to Alabama and got a divorce. You can get them quick down there."

"But what *happened*? They were so happy."

"I don't know what happened. Most of the time we were in a bar in the Village, talking about life and growth and maturity. He said he felt the need to grow. When we got around to talking about the divorce he phoned some girl and she came right over. We didn't talk about much after that."

Helen made a grimace and looked tired. "What's the new girl like?"

"She's like eighteen. She's older than that, but you know the type."

"Maybe they can grow up together."

She sat back in her chair and sipped her drink. She felt as betrayed by the Benjamins as I did. I put my empty sherry glass on the chess table; I was getting hungry.

"The Petersens have split up," she said at last. "You knew about that?"

"You said they were going to."

"Stephanie was up here a couple of weeks ago. She said the marriage was destroying her personality. She didn't know who she was any more. Men are all right, she said. Only be sure to marry the right one." Helen smiled slightly and looked over at me. "Why do people marry the wrong ones?"

"I don't know," I said. "I didn't marry the wrong one. You didn't marry the wrong one. How should we know?"

"I'm glad you're back. Did I tell you that?"

After dinner we decided to go out, but we had no place to go. I suggested a movie. Helen said she had seen it, had seen them all. We washed the dishes and finally agreed to go to a coffee house down Mount Auburn Street. Helen slid behind the curtain to her bedroom alcove. "I think I won't put on stockings or heels," she said. She pushed the curtains aside somewhat and glanced out at me. I told her that whatever she wore was all right by me. She was dressed as always, a white blouse and a tight skirt. She stood in front of a little wall mirror, jerking a brush through her hair. Then she put on lipstick, came out, and pulled the curtain shut. In all the time I had known Helen I had never seen her bed; we kept our distance. She gave me the keys to her VW and we set off.

We went to a small place called The Trap—the sign board on the door showed a rat caught by the neck—a favorite hangout for students. The air smelled of stale cigarette smoke and boiled coffee. The furniture and the walls were painted dull black; the coffee bar was on one side and on the other side there was a bare space of floor with an empty long-legged stool under a spotlight. Most of the room was in the dark, and there was only a scattering of customers. We picked a table a little way back from the spotlight, near another couple, and sat down. Helen took out a cigarette and tried to look around us without turning her head. Two young men in grubby-looking jerseys were playing checkers in a corner, and a girl at their table was watching the game with boredom. A fat boy with a sparse curly blond head was seated in a chair against the wall, gazing into the spotlight. There were some young couples in quiet conversation, and a young man in a jacket and necktie was reading a book. Helen asked me had I ever been here before; never, I said.

"Nor I. But I love the decor."

"It doesn't show the dirt."

A girl with dark glossy skin handed us the coffee list, took our order, and left. She was graceful and well built.

"She's not wearing a bra under that shift," Helen said. "And I'm willing to bet she's not wearing underpants, either."

I laughed. "Shall we leave?"

She blew some smoke in my face and turned away.

"Don't look so prim," I said. "You'll get us thrown out."

Eventually, the girl brought us our coffee. More people had come in and now a young woman with a guitar climbed onto the stool and bowed her head over the strings. The room went silent. A long spiral of gold hair uncoiled slowly over her cheek and hung dazzling in the light, then she lifted her face to us and began to sing in a soft, clear voice. After each song she waited a few moments, sometimes murmuring a couple of words to the patrons. The place was crowded and getting noisy. Helen started, turned to me. "Someone just came in I don't want to see again," she said.

A group of two men and two women were edging toward a table just in front of us. I didn't recognize anybody.

"The one in the blue jacket." She spoke quietly, keeping her eyes lowered to our table.

The one in the blue jacket was a hefty young man with short reddish hair. He saw Helen, glanced at me, then turned to look at the guitarist as she prepared to sing. "He's already seen you," I said. "Who is he?"

"He owns a yacht. Let's get out of here."

The chatter faded and the girl began to sing again. No one stirred. When she finished, the talking burst out and the man in the blue jacket stood up and came to our table. Helen sat back in her chair, looking at me.

"Hello, Helen," he said pleasantly. "Why don't you two come over and join us?"

Helen didn't answer. "We like it back here," I said.

"Skip Surrey is my name." He smiled and shot out his hand, so I shook it.

"Forgive me," Helen said. She introduced us formally. "Mr Surrey is a broker," she added. "And he's very, very rich."

He looked at me, then turned to Helen. "Is this why you don't answer your mail?"

I went to the coffee bar to pay our check just as the guitarist began another song. Surrey dropped into my chair to continue talking and Helen sat back with a cigarette, watching me. The song ended and I got back to the table.

"Try to be decent," Surrey told Helen. "For once, be decent."

She stood and snubbed out her cigarette while I put down some change for the waitress.

"You don't have to be a bitch all your life," he said hoarsely.

The two women at his first table had turned to look at us and the young man with them was trying to smile. "Easy does it, Skip," he said.

Helen edged past Surrey, then jerked sideways, and went stumbling as he groped for her leg. "Bitch!" he shouted. I stayed with him—he had fallen back into the chair with a look of misery—and when Helen reached the door I went to join her. Outside she put her arm through mine and we walked along without talking. The streets were wet and it was cooler than before. We came to her VW. "Let's keep walking," she said. She slipped her arm from mine and we continued our walk. We went down a quiet street, passed between two empty Harvard Houses, and came at last to the edge of the drive. We stopped under the trees and watched the cars flashing by and the wide black river with the broken lights on it. The air was foul with river smell. We began to walk slowly back to the car.

"It's so absolutely banal," Helen said. "He got me on board his yacht—we sat in Rockport Harbor, had one drink each—and then he tried to seduce me. I told him I wasn't having any this year and he's been out of his mind ever since. He keeps writing me letters," she added. "Financial reports and social news. Now he's engaged to be married and he says it's all my fault."

We walked slowly on the quiet street, past the long Houses with thick ivy all over the windows.

"I'm not a bitch."

"I know you're not a bitch, Helen."

"I used to sleep around," she said later. "But I don't any more."

"You're all right."

"Let's go back to my apartment. We can have a brandy."

It was still hot in the apartment. Helen went into the bathroom while I poured the brandy and set the glasses on the little chess table. Under the checkered top there was a thin drawer holding a set of hand-carved chessmen, each piece in a separate slot, with the castles mounted on the backs of tiny elephants. Some Irish grandfather had brought the table back from India and it had belonged to Helen's father who had been quite a chess player. Helen had washed her face, put on fresh lipstick, and now she stood looking out the window.

"How come you never ask me to play chess any more?" I asked.

"I don't know." She turned and half smiled. "Psychotherapy ruined my game."

We sipped brandy in the quiet.

"What are you going to do with your salary now that you've given up supporting the doctor?"

"I don't know, really. I might move to a better apartment. Maybe I'll put it in the bank, save it. I might take a trip to Europe next summer," she added vaguely.

She stretched out, rested her head against the back of the chair, and gazed at the ceiling. Her face looked pale and tired.

"We were the oldest people there tonight," she said. "I'm getting old."

"We're the same age."

"Yes. But for a woman it's about five years older." She continued to watch the ceiling. "Do you remember the time I told you I'd kill myself if I wasn't married by thirty?"

"That was a long time ago. And we were drinking beer in Cronin's. I hope you've changed your mind. You have a little while left."

"You know me better than that. I'm well behaved now. I haven't done anything rash for a long, long time." She laughed.

"You were so gallant. You tried to argue me into making a mar-riage of convenience."

"Did I offer myself?"

"That would have been incest," she said dryly. "You were will-ing to shove me off on anybody who would take me. That wasn't so gallant, now that I think about it."

We had finished our brandies. Helen asked if I wanted some more; I said no. She asked me to do her a favor, turn off the lamps.

"That's better," she murmured. "At least it looks cooler this way."

The room was gray with light from the street lamps below. She pulled off her shoes and let her head rest on the back of the chair again. The music of a dance band floated up to the windows over the swish and swish of automobiles, then it faded. It was quiet briefly, then more automobiles swept past.

"We don't write any more," she said after a time.

About a year ago Helen had fallen in love with someone named Thomas Leverett; she was talking about him.

"It's probably just as well," I said. She was silent for a long while and I couldn't see whether she had her eyes open or closed.

"I think I would have made a good mother," she said at last. She was probably thinking of Leverett's daughter.

"You will. You'll have your own."

"The State Department sent him to Geneva. He wrote just be-fore he left. He took his daughter with him. She's thirteen, did you know that?"

"No. I didn't know that."

"Well," she said a bit later. "You and I didn't marry the wrong ones."

"That's something."

"It's not much, but it's something." She was silent a while. "I think it's time you went home," she said.

I said I thought she was right. We got up and walked cautiously through the shadows to the door. She squinted in the glare from the hallway, then she smiled gently, and we said good night. Outside the air was mild, and it was pleasant to have the long walk back to my apartment.

5

My father is not a talkative man. He is a civil engineer, a builder of highways and bridges and towers, but if you ask him he will tell you that he is a surveyor, just a surveyor. He was born in 1899 in South Boston and when he was four his parents took him on a trip to their home town, Morano, in the province of Cosenza, in Calabria on the toe of Italy. He remembers the lamps, little clay shells filled with oil in which floated a softly burning wick, and the cows and chickens came into the house to sleep. Back in Boston he went to Quincy Grammar School; during the summer he swam in Fort Point Channel, and winters he skated on Boston Common and bought freshly roasted chestnuts to stuff into his mittens against the cold walk home. Later he went to Mechanic Arts High School, for during one summer he had worked as rodman on a surveying team and now he wanted to be a surveyor. After he graduated from high school he began work for the Pontone Construction Company, taking courses in his free time at the Wentworth Institute. Later he married my mother and after the wedding trip when he walked into Mr. Pontone's office to ask for a raise in pay Mr. Pontone made him a partner in the company.

When I was a boy what impressed me most about my father was

his knowledge and his penmanship. Whenever I asked him a question he knew the answer and it was right. He could add up long columns of numbers and never make a mistake. Whenever he used his pen the writing was clean; the words never came out cramped or broken in little bits, never tipped slantwise on the paper but always went along on a level line with all the letters straight up and down. He could write numerals freehand that looked like they were printed in an arithmetic table, and whenever he wanted especially to see something he would draw a line at it and when he took the pencil away there would be a little arrowhead on the end of the line, pointing. At home he had a study where you could not go unless he was inside and gave permission. He had a desk with a green blotter and a long black table covered with blueprints, and a dark bookcase with glass doors that opened with a key. On his desk there was an ivory slide rule inscribed with rows of tiny numbers that counted backward and forward, getting squeezed together at the ends, and a glass square with a hair in it. Sometimes he would unlock the bookcase and show me the flat box with his drawing instruments. The outside was hard black leather, rough as pebbles, and inside was glorious blue velvet with the silver dividers and compasses glittering like jewelry. He could draw perfect circles with a little twist of his fingers, or circles inside of circles inside of circles, triangles, diamonds, stars, willow leaves, flowers, and sunbursts. One morning my father took me with him on a surveying job. Before anyone was out of bed we drove to the company to pick up his transit—the three legs tipped with spear points, the theodolite arrayed like a sundial crowned by a short brass telescope—then drove out of the city to the woods. When I woke up again the automobile had stopped in a field and my father was outside talking with some men. I got out and my father introduced me. They were wearing riding breeches and heavy boots, and one had a US canteen and a pinched hat like a soldier. My father sat on the running board to lace his boots while the others moved across the field toward the trees, carrying rods and chains and a roll of canvas and a little three-legged table. You could feel the adventure, but my father told me to stick with him and not bother anybody. The others had halted by the stream at the edge of the woods and they began to string up the canvas to make a shelter. It was exciting. My father's hands made a mistake threading his boot, then he cursed and tore out the lacing and began again. At last he drew the transit from the car, resting it on his shoulder, and we set off through the long, wet grass to join the others and begin the survey. That day my father was king and I was prince and all the wild world was our domain. When the work was done and the land lay open and known, then the heated air was yellow with dust and we returned to the cars, headed back to the city, and did not arrive home until it was dim and the street lamps were on. We had a late supper, and after my bath I lay in bed with a dream of me and my father in the fields by the woods, unafraid, and I fell asleep.

My father has never told stories about himself except in slight phrases here and there—once when I came indoors from skating he cupped my hand in both of his, lifting it to his mouth to breathe warm air, soft and melting, into my stiffened fingers, then told me about the hot chestnuts in his mittens—and he has spoken even less about his own father. As far as I know, my father's father came off a ship, then bought a box of cigars and walked to Boston Common and began selling them. Somebody ran up and knocked the box from his hand, and after that he became a storekeeper. He worked hard and prospered, then died the year before I was born. One afternoon my father and I were alone together—he had just bought me a suit—and as we drove homeward he turned the car from the thoroughfare to a quieter street, then turned again and drove into a long shadow, an alley walled with brick apartments so dark they looked as if they had been rubbed with a pencil. The street lamps were clear glass jars with iron crowns on them; the sidewalks were empty and the doorsteps were smooth as beach stones. Everything was dead quiet. "I used to live here," my father said. He had brought the car almost to a halt. "And my father used to have his store over there." I looked around, trying to make out what he had pointed at. "Where did you live?" I asked. "On the second floor." He was looking at a row of windows, the sills worn like whetstones, but I could not see which ones he meant. Already the car had begun to roll on. "Where? Where was the store?" The walls were sliding to the back of us. "Back there." But he was looking ahead and we slowly turned a corner. "Let's go home now," he said. All I had seen was a plate-glass window filled with brown paper boxes. We paused at the edge of the rushing traffic, then turned into the sunlight and noise, joined the other automobiles, and drove home.

My grandmother was a small woman in black, her hands pummeling a mound of yellow dough that spread out to almost cover the table, while everyone crowded around her with a continuous hubbub over the twisted cake ring, and the air was filled with warm bakery odors. When it was Easter the cake was shaped like a basket and there were big sugar eggs with a window at one end so you could see the rabbit inside on the flowers. On Christmas Eve there were eels in the kitchen sink, long glistening brown snakes, whipping and thrashing in frantic circles as the boiling water poured over them. The eels were served for dinner—*capitone* they called them—fried gold brown, dusted with dried herb leaves, and laid out in a long oval dish edged with yellow lemon slices, but I was sickened by the sight and took only soup and crackers, then left the table to stand in the doorway of the dim front parlor, looking at the Christmas tree in its pale luminous cloud of colored lights. Then the time came when we visited her every Sunday and we were silent in the car and if I complained that I was going to be bored by no one to play with, my father would say, "Keep quiet, Frank." When we arrived I would stay outside to play in the sun with a tennis ball and afterward I would come in to sit in the empty front parlor: a chill and gloomy room of unused furniture, stiff bulges of green bristling cloth edged with glittering dark wood, and an unused fireplace of white marble surmounted by a clock.

The clock was of polished black stone with a round glass door over its golden dial and ornate hands which had ceased to move long ago. After a while I was called to the dining room for milk and store-bought cake with the grownups, my parents talking to an aunt and uncle I did not really know—the uncle whose face was gray with weekend stubble, wearing a buttoned sweater with pale, baggy elbows, the aunt with thin shoulders and a faded apron —and the boy cousin and girl cousin who were too old to play with. They were all speaking Italian, because I could understand my mother and she was speaking Italian, but when the others spoke the sounds were strange and out of tune. At last my parents stood up, then everyone stood up and we prepared to leave. Someone gently woke my grandmother who was drowsing in her rocking chair in the corner by the hall. My mother took me out to the hall and knelt to smooth my clothes—"Now be sure to kiss Nanna good-by," she whispered—then straightening up she joined us to the others around my grandmother. When Nanna found me inside the circle all the talking stopped and everyone paused while Nanna and I looked at each other. I saw a little old woman sitting in a tall rocking chair. Her face was crumpled and blurred with wrinkles; she had soft brown eyes and a black smudge of mustache and her hands, trembling toward my face, looked as brittle and cold as porcelain. I did not want to kiss her—my insides recoiled and I shut my eyes. The hands on my face were warm and painfully gentle. We kissed. Her hands trembled back into her narrow lap and I was free to go. Her eyes were watery now.

One morning my mother said to me, "Nanna died last night. You can go out and play now, but you must remember to be very quiet when Dad comes home." I went up to my room and told myself, *Nanna is dead, Nanna is dead, Nanna is dead,* searching for the grief of those words until suddenly I burst into tears. Whether I was crying because she had suffered death, or for a pain in me, or for my father who had no mother now, I did not know. That evening my father appeared at the table wearing a black necktie I had never seen. His face was unmarked but he did not talk to me, spoke only a few words to my mother, and took for dinner a bowl of that hot clear soup which she brewed for me whenever I was sick. He did not speak of his mother and I knew I must not ask him. Whenever I tried to picture my grandmother the vision came most clearly of the house where she had lived: that long wooden building painted a green so dark it was almost black, the tall narrow end facing the street with drawn parlor shades and a high pointed roof, the square rooms going back from the chill front parlor to the hallway to the dining room to the kitchen, warm and odorous with Easter baking. I have never seen it again. The house and my grandmother and whatever uncles or aunts or cousins were in it all vanished into my father's silence.

6

My mother says that a good family means a good life; if you have a good family you have the world, and if you have no family you should begin one. She was born in 1906 in the North End of Boston, in the apartment over her father's store, and spent her first weeks swaddled in blankets in a dresser drawer on the floor, beside her mother's bed, where she was looked at by an older brother and sister. As a child she was guided and instructed by the good Sisters of Notre Dame, at their Academy outside Boston, and later by the faculty of the Reale Educatorio Maria Adelaide in Palermo. At home she looked after six younger brothers and sisters, and at school she helped to sneak vinegar into the instructor's wine glass, threw confetti on the governess's wig, and one evening she raced with her classmates round and round the courtyard under a fiery sunset, crying, *The end of the world is coming, the end of the world!* In the villa on Via Imperatore Federico she had a piano teacher, and a young tutor who wrote poems and liked to say, "One of these is by Leopardi and the other by me—now, which is which?" She went to the museums in Naples and Rome, the galleries in Florence; summers she attended the University of Palermo, and each winter the family took a box at Il

Massimo. Her father bought a big house in Washington, Massachusetts, and one by one the family came back to live there. She went to Symphony, to tea dances, and met young men. During the last winter she used to stand in the foyer and watch the snowy avenue from behind the narrow leaded windows, waiting for my father to arrive in his automobile, then she would slip back into the reception hall and stand over the hot-air vent as he came up the front steps.

My mother's parents are dead but she sees them now and again in dreams; sometimes the dreams are on the night after Christmas or Easter, sometimes after a baptism or other family gathering. One morning I asked what age her mother and father were in the dreams, how old they looked, and she said, "Frank, dear, my father was a vigorous man and looked the same his whole life." I asked what color his beard was in the dream. "I don't remember—he shaved it off once but we made him grow it again—and my mother's hair was black, like mine used to be." I can remember my grandfather thrusting his beard against my cheek, roaring and laughing; his vest was scratchy, smelled of cigars, and he liked to push my face into it. I distrusted him. Once, in the big house in Washington, he said for me to come with him down into the wine cellar. He opened a door in the kitchen and went ahead of me down a shuddering stairway, down past gray stones and stringy cobwebs, into the cool dark air. I heard the rattling of a door, the damp odor of bare earth came out, then he returned with a lighted candle to lead me in by the hand. I wanted to get out. He drew the wine through a funnel with a trickling sound, and when the bottle was full he poked it at me. "Drink it. Go ahead. It won't hurt you." He watched until I swallowed a mouthful, then he roared and slapped my back again and again. I was sick with fear. He corked the bottle and dropped it into his jacket pocket, swept me suddenly over his shoulder, and after jouncing up the stairway, set me on my feet in the kitchen. Afterward we all went aboard a ship where you could taste salt if you licked the rail, then we went back on the pier and watched my grandfather go to Sicily. My mother often spoke of her parents, but they were not around and I did not think about them. Then one morning I was brought to meet my grandmother. She was huge. She had white hair, a large tanned face, and she wore a black dress stretched tight over something like a barrel. Her arms and breasts stuck out at the top, her legs bulged and descended crosswise into a pair of tiny shoes which seemed about to burst. She gave a mournful cry and opened her arms while I was pressed forward to kiss her—she was soft and smelled of lemon—then she wept briefly, dried her eyes, and began talking excitedly to my parents about her voyage. Later my grandmother unfolded a large blue cloth, shaking it so it billowed and rippled, then as it ebbed on the table she smoothed out the wrinkles and said to me, "This is where your grandfather lives." In the middle was a big green triangle: a map of Sicily. She touched the cloth with her fingers, her pale almond nails, pointing. There were steamships and sailboats in the Mediterranean, embroidered gardens with bunches of grapes and oranges and figs on the land, olive trees and palms, little villages sewn on the edge of the water, and Mount Etna with red threads blazing from its top. She said that my grandfather was coming as soon as he could find a ship. During the next few months I expected him, waited uneasily, but he never arrived and after a while I forgot all about him. Later I came to realize that my grandfather had not booked passage soon enough and that the war, which was on now, had marooned him in Palermo. Then we lived with my grandmother in the big house in Washington, and I learned about my grandfather, his store on Prince Street in the North End, his factories, his apartment houses, his bank, and the villa on the Via Imperatore Federico. The house in Washington had a white pillared porch which curved around one side, a carriage house in the rear, a *boccie* court laid with fine blue gravel, and its pride was a double stairway which ascended from the reception hall back to a landing beneath two windows twelve feet tall, then vanished forward to the second floor. We occupied the first two floors, rented out the third-floor servants' quarters and the carriage house. "The income barely pays the coal man, let alone the tax collector, and everyone in town thinks we're rich," said my father.

In the villa on Via Imperatore Federico the dining room opened onto a large balcony and we used to have our meals there. The wall behind the balcony was faced with blue glazed tile, overhead was a grape trellis, and along the sides were slatted bamboo curtains which could be rolled down for shade. We looked out over the garden and beyond the walls to La Favorita and the Villa Airoldi and beyond that to the towering yellow-brown rock of Monte Pellegrino. In the evening it was pleasant to stay at the table while the sky faded and the air grew cool. There was my grandmother—she was larger than ever before, had burst her corsets and discarded them, and now wore a loose tentlike garment which looked comfortable—and her oldest daughter, Regina, and Regina's daughter Felicia, and Felicia's daughter, Angelica. Also there was Mario, Aunt Regina's friend; he came to say a few words to the family who rented the top floor or to listen to complaints about the housekeeper, to give orders to the caretaker, stroll in the garden, and have dinner, then rattle the doors, lock the gate, and drive away to his own apartment. One night I asked him why nothing grew in the garden, my mother always talked about the figs and the orange trees. "Mario didn't get the garden pipes fixed. That's why we have no oranges this year," Aunt Regina broke in.

"Why should I spend your aunt's money to get the pipes fixed?" Mario asked me gently. "She couldn't afford to pay for the water."

Felicia had come onto the balcony with a shawl for my grandmother. "Mario has a mind that goes from the front of his store to the back, no further," she said. She turned on the wall light and went back inside.

The bickering made me uneasy and I shifted my chair to look out at the horizon. The sky was pale on one side and black on the other and Monte Pellegrino was beginning to look flat as a shadow. Regina went inside, saying, "Come in soon, mamà. It's getting cool." A few moments later Mario rubbed out his cigar, patted my shoulder, and went in, too. "Everyone talks too much," my grandmother said later. I turned to face her. "Have a little more wine," she added, pushing the bottle toward me. "Your grandfather died right here on this balcony. He had just bought a ship from the United States Navy. He was happy."

"He bought a ship? From the Navy? The United States sold him a ship?"

"A ship—the kind you carry things in—a little freighter. He was going to ship things around the Mediterranean."

I asked my grandmother what happened next, but she seemed to have lost interest.

"He loved this balcony," she said. "We had just finished dinner, finished the dessert. He asked for another dish of sherbet." She sighed. "I went in, and when I came out with the sherbet he was dead." She began to weep.

I called Aunt Regina and we helped my grandmother to her feet. She brushed aside our hands, paused, then moved painfully to the door. She put one hand on Regina and the other on the door jamb, heaved herself onto the threshold, hesitated, then disappeared into the dim room followed by my aunt.

My grandmother had nine children, eight when she died:

Aurelio, the first born and a son, was swept from his horse by a low tree branch; he died young.

Regina, the first daughter, married a landowner with a lien on a title of Sicilian nobility, divorced, divested herself of all except her child and her husband's fancy name; she transformed herself from seamstress to mannequin to shopkeeper to dress designer; surviving the Fascists, the United States Air Force, and the Allied invasion, she emerged as a translator in US Army Headquarters, Palermo, and went on to become an executive secretary, black marketeer, and—after the war—*couturiere,* dealer in pearls and semi-precious stones, landowner, *rentiere,* passing on to her daughter her survival techniques and that disused title which had been held in escrow for more than thirty years.

Maria; she's my mother.

Cesare (USMC), quick and handsome and brave and arrogant, went to the South Pacific, married, and came back divorced, made a fortune in New York and lost it in Paris, made another in Rome and lost it in Caracas; he now owns part of a vineyard in upstate New York: "At least my relatives won't call it another get-rich-quick scheme," he says.

Firenze married a journeyman printer who worked hard, bought his own press, and became almost prosperous by printing cards, handbills, pamphlets, yearbooks, and an occasional volume of poetry; then he designed his own type face, turned his savings into matrices and fonts, and went broke promoting an arcane beauty which people might look at but never see, let alone appreciate or admire.

Marco (USAF) married an English woman.

Elena-Bianca, the intellectual, ran off with a Neapolitan whom she had met six months earlier at a Circolo Italiano dance, a scholar who possessed the clothes he married in plus a suitcase packed with volumes of Dante, Petrarch, Tasso, Boccaccio, and his own poems; she worked as a secretary while he taught in a private academy for rich boys, then as a typist while he studied at a graduate school, back and forth for half a dozen years until he surfaced as an instructor in philosophy, enabling them thirty years later to enjoy the sparse but secure luxuries endowed him as chairman of a four-man department in a country college.

Dante (USA) married a good woman, works hard, and prospers; they have the most children, all girls and at last one boy.

Isolda, whom I fell in love with at six, was married at eighteen and widowed at twenty-two, became first a real-estate agent, then a land speculator, finally a professional gambler: beautiful but not very lucky.

In Harvard Square one evening I stopped to look through a newspaper and came across an obituary for my grandmother. She had died in the villa in Palermo. I went to a street phone and called my parents. My father told me that they had received the cablegram from Aunt Regina last night and had sent a note to the newspapers. My mother sounded tired and her voice wavered. I tried to say something about our own family, said I would be home to visit them soon, then hung up. I felt as if a rope had been cut through, cast off like a mooring.

7

Scott was president of Research/Research, his wife Alice was treasurer, and a lawyer friend of theirs whom I have shaken hands with at a cocktail party was clerk. The corporation made money by selling information. If you wanted to know something about communications, R and R would gather and edit reports, make abstracts, compile bibliographies and personnel lists, give advice. R and R sometimes hired consultants from Harvard and the Massachusetts Institute of Technology, or paid graduate students to do library work and to draft reports, but the heart and brains of the outfit was Scott himself. He had a doctorate in physics from MIT, had worked for the Radio Corporation of America, American Telephone, Lincoln Labs, and the Institute for Defense Analyses. Two years ago he had come to Cambridge and set up Research/Research. He seemed to know everyone he needed to know and to have a clairvoyant sense of communications technology. Marian was his secretary and I was his rewrite man, his drudge. I had a good office: a small room with pale walls, a couple of chairs and a desk, a redwood bookshelf, a coat rack, and two windows. The windows had drapes made of white fish nets and I could look across our gravel drive into the dim interior of the house next door, or out to the sidewalk and Brattle Street. I have in mind a bright morning when the leaves lay yellow and red in the driveway and the women on Brattle Street walked briskly, wearing thin coats and tan leather gloves. I was trying to get through a report by a man named Steiner, a graduate student at the Massachusetts Institute of Technology. I had spent my freshman and sophomore years at MIT and then had quit to go to the Rhode Island School of Design, so Steiner looked upon me as a scientist who had not made good, a failure. Steiner liked to number his paragraphs and to capitalize certain honorable words, like engineer or physicist; it was slow reading. I heard a gentle rap-rap on the door between my room and Scott's office. Scott was in his shirt sleeves, wearing glasses, and he looked glum. "What's wrong with Marian?" he murmured.

"Is something wrong?"

He glanced at the door from my office to the outside room where we could hear Marian typing, then back to me. "I gave her a two-page letter to type and she forgot the second page. She put my name at the bottom of page one and brought it in for me to sign. When I pointed out that she had omitted the last few paragraphs she burst into tears. Am I supposed to thank her for her mistakes?" he whispered.

"She has her period today. She's been knocking things off her desk all morning."

Scott paused, stared at me. Then he sighed. "She tells you when she has her period?"

"She told me she had cramps. She's very regular."

"Maybe I should jot it down on my calendar." He lowered himself carefully into the chair beside my desk. "Maybe I can arrange to be out of town a month from now."

"Why don't you give her the day off?"

"Oh, no. If I go out there and tell her she can go home she'll start crying. I know that much." He took off his glasses. "I suppose we should be grateful that she's on time. I hope my daughters are as regular."

"Is that something you worry about?"

"The two older ones are safe enough, I guess. At least they're married. But I don't know about Heather."

"Heather looks like a sensible girl." Heather had visited our offices just before she left for college, a tall girl with a quick smile and bright eyes. She was taller than I was, actually.

"She doesn't trust me. The last message she sent was a postcard. 'Have arrived safe and sound, Heather.' She never tells me anything." He looked sullen.

"What do you want? She's twenty-one. She has her own life to lead. Why should she confide in you?"

"No. No. You don't understand. I don't expect her to tell me secrets. But she doesn't trust me. After her mother died she stopped talking to me. We used to have long talks together, just the two of us." Scott's first wife had died about five years ago.

"She's grown up now. Why don't you leave her alone?"

"She's my daughter."

"That explains everything. You should have put her in a convent."

"It explains more than you know." His voice was loud and abrupt. "More than you'll ever know if you're lucky." Suddenly his face was swollen, mottled pink and white.

"All right, Scott. All right."

"What if she turns out like that?" he muttered, jerking his head toward the outside room, toward Marian. "This is her last year in college and I'd like to know what she plans to do."

"She probably hasn't got any plans. Maybe she'll get married and live happily ever after."

"I hope so."

"Did you finish laying those flagstones?" Scott had been building a patio to his home out in Lincoln. He had started the job months ago.

"Yes. Much to my surprise." He relaxed. "You ought to come out sometime. I have about a cord of wood which needs to be chopped. Maybe I can get some work out of you."

"Thanks."

"What are you reading?"

"Steiner." I turned the book toward Scott. He put on his glasses and looked at the page skeptically for a few moments, then shrugged and turned it back to me.

"That's what I pay you for," he said. He put his hands to the arms of the chair and eased himself upward. "Can you come out to dinner sometime?"

"Anytime."

"I'll tell Alice." He moved into his office, closing the door slowly and quietly with a little click.

I stretched, got up, and walked around the room for a while. I took off my necktie, put it inside my jacket, and hung the jacket on the coat rack, then I opened the window a bit. The air was chill but not cold. I slumped back in the chair, put my heels on the top edge of the lowest drawer, and began reading Steiner again. Sometime later Scott knocked on our door. He had his jacket on, his raincoat over his arm, his brief case in hand; he said he was going out to Hanscom Field. "Have a good lunch," I said. When I finished reading I opened the door to the outer room. Marian was typing a letter. The air was rich, thick with orange-blossom perfume. I strolled around, looking out the front windows at the streams of people on Brattle Street. I asked Marian was she going out to lunch soon.

"I'm not hungry," she said. She removed the letter, inserted an envelope, began typing. The skin under her eyes was discolored, brown.

"Why don't you go out anyway? Get some fresh air. Go out with Hanne." Hanne was Ibera's new secretary, a Danish girl; he had found her about a month ago.

"Hanne is going out to lunch with her young man."

"What young man?"

"Her Harvard young man. A grad student. He even speaks Danish." She switched off her typewriter, slipped the letter under the envelope flap, and fastened them together with a paper clip.

"I thought you *liked* Hanne."

"I do."

"Well, you sound like you could murder her."

"Frank, you have a *vivid* imagination."

I began winding the clock on the fireplace mantel. Marian cleared her desk, then bent down and pulled open the bottom drawer. From the drawer she had taken a novel, tossing it onto the desk; now she searched further into the drawer and drew out a glittering bottle of whisky. She sat up, flushed. "How about a drink?" she asked.

"For the cramps?"

"The only remedy, the pain killer that never fails." She stood the bottle on the desk and began picking at the seal with her blunt red nails. "Well, don't you want a drink?" she pleaded. "Be a gentleman and join me, say yes."

"Yes. But I want to eat first. Why don't I get us some food?"

"All right. You go out, bring back some sandwiches for yourself, then we can drink. Because I'm not hungry."

I went up the street to Max's and bought a couple of big hot pastrami sandwiches. I figured I could get Marian to eat one of them. The sky was blue as ice, but the air was not chill any longer. Everyone looked pleased, excited. When I came back Marian was reading her novel and there were two coffee mugs alongside the bottle. "It's a beautiful day," I said. "Let's go out back." I gathered up the bottle and mugs while Marian locked and rattled Scott's door, locked her desk and the filing cabinets, then we stepped into the hall and she locked the big office door behind us. At the far end of the hallway was a door which led onto the back yard; we went out and left it open. Ibera had the lawn mowed and raked every couple of weeks during the summer, but it was shaggy now and I liked it. We sat on the wooden bench that ran around the trunk of the crab-apple tree. I unwrapped the sandwiches while Marian poured whisky into the mugs. I offered a sandwich to Marian, but she said she wasn't hungry. "Eat it while it's still hot," I told her. She shook her head, crossed her legs, and leaned back against the tree, sipping her mug of whisky. "It will go to waste," I said. "And it's a sin to waste food."

"That's your problem, lover."

I rewrapped Marian's sandwich and began eating mine. It tasted good. The slugs of whisky now and again were strange, but not bad. It was peaceful to sit there eating and not talking, just looking at the grass or the dusty gravel walk or the back of the house. The shingles gleamed in the sun and you could see inside the second-story windows.

"What do you suppose Ibera does up there?" Marian asked.

"Haven't you ever gone upstairs? Those are his drafting rooms. He has some slaves chained up there who do all his detail work."

"Oh?"

"How did Hanne meet her young man?"

"Don't ask me. She came over from Denmark for a summer visit and then decided to stay. So she took this job with Ibera and met her young man. Love at first sight." Marian took a big swallow of whisky, wincing. She turned to me. "If you had plans for her I think you're too late. Besides," she added, "Ibera's secretaries always get married."

"I plan to get married."

"Who doesn't?"

We didn't talk for a long while. The old bench was made of unpainted wood, silver with age, and it was warm. The gravel at our feet was scattered with small yellow apples and there were leaves, ovals and crescents, speckled with yellow and black. The big elms over the street were just about empty, bearing a few brown leaves. Later I offered Marian the remaining pastrami sandwich, but she turned it away. I asked her how she was feeling.

"Awful," she said. "Like an old bag. Which I am. I have the worst menstrual pains of anyone I know. I die once a month."

"Why don't you go to a doctor?"

"I did. He gave me some pills but they didn't do any good. They made me groggy. I kept falling asleep. I tried them for three months and I spent a week in bed each month, sleeping. Then he gave me some other pills that made me so dizzy I threw up."

I finished my whisky. "Where does it hurt?"

"Down here," she said, rubbing her stomach. "And way down in my back. Like I'm having a baby. It feels like what they say labor pains are like. But it's worse, because when it's all over you don't have anything. Not a fucking thing." Her hair was bushed out and her eyes were puffy; she looked real haggard.

"Why don't you take the afternoon off?"

"Doctors like to say it's all in your mind. They tell you that whenever they can't cure something, especially if you're a woman."

I could not find much to say, so finally I kept quiet. I guessed that if Marian wanted to take the afternoon off she would take it off, and if she wanted to stay in the office that was her business. I finished half of the remaining sandwich and wrapped up the rest.

"Kevin is all right," she said. "It's his mother who blocks progress. That lovely lady is seventy-three years old."

"Let him get you pregnant. Force him to marry you."

She turned and looked at me, wounded. "Is that a nice thing to say? Is that what you think of me?"

"I was only joking."

"Well," she said. "Anyway, if you knew Kevin you wouldn't dream of such advice." She stood up, holding the whisky bottle in one hand and the mug in the other. "Coming in?"

8

I put my feet on the bottom drawer and slumped down in my chair to watch the people walking past on Brattle Street. I had always enjoyed looking at people, and had done it for hours on end in the past, but recently I had been unable to keep my old interest in it. I had come around to seeing that the appointments those others hurried toward, the meetings and conferences, the assignations were never for me; the men had business to conduct, or adventure perhaps, the stylish women were completely taken care of, the young girls sailed buoyantly onward to others. It would never matter to them, or to anyone at all, that I was here as witness, and no one was going to turn and smile and wave, invite me to a fresher world. My eyes got tired of following this or that face, grew confused, dizzy, muddled. I was left out, left behind. I was lonely. Later I took a stroll around the outer office. Marian had arranged some open notebooks on her desk and had set a half-typed page in the typewriter. She was reading her novel, improving herself. She asked if I had any typing for her; I said no. I told her I was going to see if Ibera wanted to go out for coffee, then I went across the hall. Ibera's offices were laid out somewhat like ours, but he had only two rooms on the floor and others upstairs. One wall had photographs of a house he had designed—a long glass box on stilts—and in a corner there was a model of the same house on a little table under a plastic dome. Hanne Helmsen, Ibera's secretary, was seated at her desk turning the pages of a dictionary. Hanne had this thick stream of gold hair which descended through a wooden clasp at the back of her head. She looked up, smiled. "Ah, Frank, how are you today?" Her accent was delightful. I said I was fine and asked her how she was. Oh, she was very fine, she said. I asked her was Ibera in. She said no, and she looked really dismayed. "But I can help you?" Then Harvey Wilson stuck his head in from the next room and asked did I want to go out for coffee, distracting me.

"Is Marian very busy, do you know?" Hanne asked.

"I don't think she's busy," I said.

Hanne stood up and tucked the back of her blouse deeper into her skirt—she had grand breasts—and took her dictionary across the hall. Wilson and I headed out to Max's.

"You *did* want to go out for coffee, didn't you?" he asked as we walked up the street.

"What else?"

Wilson glanced at me, curious. "How's the job?"

"I don't like to work for other people."

"Scott pays well, you said."

"I give him my time and he gives me money. It's a bad bargain, and I lose in the end."

The sun was warm, but you could feel the cold whenever you walked through a shadow. Wilson took a deep gulp of air and smiled. He had a handsome body and a habit of wearing white sneakers, and he always looked like he was trotting onto some playing field. He was one of Ibera's builders.

"Why don't you come to dinner tonight?" he asked.

"I could take you up on that."

"I'm serious. What do you say?"

"I'd be bad company, very morose." I liked Harvey Wilson, liked his pretty wife and his two small daughters, and I enjoyed having dinner with them, but I always felt more lonely than ever when I had to go home. I had given up trying to explain these things.

"Don't brood so much," he said. "Just come and eat." In a while he would suggest that I get married.

"Not tonight."

"Have it your way. Anytime, you know."

"Thanks," I said. We pushed into Max's and stood at the counter, waiting for our coffee. I happened to see Gretta Anders putting on her coat. Gretta was a tall, thin girl whose hair was so blond it was almost white, what they call ash blond. When she saw me she smiled and we exchanged hellos as she went out. She was a striking girl, though somewhat rangy.

"Who was *that?*" Wilson asked.

"That was Miss Anders. She belongs to a friend of mine."

"Why don't you get married and suffer like the rest of us?"

"All my friends are getting divorced."

He grunted. "I think I'll get a divorce, too. From Ibera."

"Again?" Every few months Ibera and Wilson had a fight and decided not to do business with each other. Ibera once told me that Wilson couldn't put two toy blocks together without finding a way to run the cost up ten per cent.

"Ibera should have been an interior decorator," Wilson went on. "Then he wouldn't have to worry about plumbing or wiring or where to put the goddamn heater. I won't bore you with the details of this last mess."

"Bore me," I said.

The coffee arrived and we sat in a booth where Wilson gave me all the details. It wasn't so boring, and it passed the time. Afterward Wilson climbed into his ruin of a station wagon and drove off someplace, while I walked back to the office.

Marian had put her novel aside and was typing. Her hair was neatly combed, she looked more cheerful. "Scott telephoned to say that he was going directly home. He's not going to be in till tomorrow. Also, the Fargo building called and left no message." I thanked her and went into my room. I rolled down my sleeves, buttoned the cuffs, put on my jacket, and sat at my desk. I felt like I was going to drop dead of loneliness. I came out to see what time it was. The clock on the fireplace mantel had been brought over from Paris by Scott. It was in a slender glass box: the works and the dial were in the top half, and a gold wire hung straight down, suspending four thin spokes, each with a gold ball on the end. I watched as the wire twisted very slowly around to the left, hesitated, than untwisted and twisted very slowly around to the right, hesitated, then untwisted and— Marian stopped typing and looked up at me a moment with her soft, haggard eyes. "Why don't you go out for a walk?" she suggested.

9

When the air grew chill I turned from the banks of the river and walked up Boylston Street to Harvard Square. The lights were coming on and the sky looked frail, thin, almost transparent. The Square was crowded, people overflowing the sidewalks, streaming in among cars and taxis. I headed down to my apartment to prepare supper. As I walked along, Sophia Alden slid behind the wheel of her car, then she saw me and waved excitedly. Sophia was thirty-five and some years old, not bad looking. She leaned across the front seat and rolled down the window. "Frank," she cried. "It's so good to *see* you. How long have you been back in town?"

I told her that I had not been back long.

"We ought to get together some evening. Don't be shy. I finally bought a TV." She smiled at me, then touched her black gloved hand to the door of the automobile. "Can I give you a ride someplace?"

I said no, told her I was going to my apartment, just down the street.

"Let me give you a lift," she suggested.

I thanked her and said no again.

"Ah, well." She smiled, crinkling the corners of her eyes. She turned the key and the motor started purring. "Do come by," she said. I stepped back and waved good-by. She turned her head, peering out into the traffic, and the car swung slowly away from the curb. I had met her at some cocktail party, then had forgotten her and met her again; it turned out we knew some of the same people. Sophia smiled and waved her fingers at me, then roared off.

After Alba and I broke up, I wandered around and in the middle of winter I went to look over a teaching job in a small private school tucked away in the country. The buildings which housed the school had been built more than a hundred years ago by a group of men and women who had come together from all parts of the Eastern States and had journeyed to the slopes of this little valley to stake out a community, a little township, where they would live in such a way as they believed would bring about God's kingdom on earth. I once read some of the pamphlets which this society of believers printed up about themselves. They had a little rule book, as simply worded as a carpenter's manual, by which they ordered their daily life. There were only a few rules and these were quite exact—such as which shoe to put on first in the morning, or which thumb to place over which when they folded their hands to pray—but they were so snugly joined, each to each, that if you followed them from hour to hour you could not stray so far as to bump into anything not treated in the little book. They wrote in a simple and concise way about their daily lives and quite simply even of some extraordinary happenings—such as when two bright angels burst into their meeting house and soared over the assembly—but their most sacred books were dictated to them by voices speaking a passionate metaphorical rhetoric which I could not grasp, and I was never able to learn precisely what they did believe.

They worked hard. It is clear from everything they said and did that they sensed the time of God's arrival was now drawing near. They were diffident about figuring the precise date—perhaps they felt it would have been presumptuous to schedule His arrival too closely—and they spoke of His coming with delicate reticence and tact, as you might speak of an honored guest who has as yet failed to show up. They were filled with gloomy optimism. Each one privately mounted guard, kept an eye out for God, and worked energetically toward the unknown date of His coming. They broke open the fields and plowed them. They chopped down the forest, sawed it into boards to season for the day when it would be measured off, cut, planed, and nailed down tight; they planted neat orchards of apple and pear. They hacked a quarry out of the mountain side, split it into blocks to be squared off and later set in place so snugly that you couldn't drive a nail between any two of them, and they built a barn and a meeting house and several dormitories. They set up a saw mill, dug a storage cellar for potatoes, and built a round stone silo for corn. They pulled out stumps and dragged away boulders; they leveled the hillocks, straightened out roads, laid stone walks, and planted flat lawns.

But all this gave them no joy. They labored with dread. At times they seemed to be working not merely with zeal but with tight-lipped panic, and it is hard to tell whether they felt they were preparing a day so that God would come, or whether they sensed the moment of His arrival was almost on them and they were desperately trying to get things in order. Already they felt the first tremors of His presence and each day they lifted their eyes warily to the towering horizon and to the steep clouds where at any moment He might be spied gathering up His robes, setting His toe cautiously upon a mountain top, about to come striding into their valley. The seasons passed but He never showed up. They continued to work hard, not so much with desperation now as with stubbornness and at last with pride and almost with bitterness, and the community prospered.

They were determined to be a self-sustaining, God-reliant village. They wanted to do as much as possible by themselves and to do as little as possible with the rest of the world. They added a smithy, enlarged the saw mill to include a carpentry shop, and built a mill to grind corn. They were polite to the neighboring villagers who came over to watch them every now and then, but they had few dealings with them and struck up no friendships. When they found they needed something—iron, glass, cotton—they bartered for it, for they had grown expert at wood and metal crafts and were always able to trade articles of woodwork or wrought iron for so many square inches of glass or bales of cotton. They had no need of money, but they took as much solid cash as they could get for grinding corn, and bought more land. The general stores in the surrounding towns filled up with machine-made articles—gadgets which began to fall apart as soon as they were put together—but they continued to work by hand, and in time they became well known and admired for their skill in making chairs and wrought-iron fixtures, such as door latches, hinges, and tiny boxlike stoves. There was a barren geometric beauty in the style of their handiwork. Their famous rocking chairs, lean curves of almost inflexible wood held together by wooden pegs, resembled an Indian bow with a sheaf of unfeathered arrows, and their wrought-iron door latches, trimmed down to an appearance of fragility, worked with delicate but firm precision. The outside villagers held that the settlers were stingy and tightfisted, and that the thin elegance of their workmanship was the result of their searching out the best way to make a boot-scraper with the least amount of iron.

The outside townspeople had begun to resent the community. They didn't care one way or the other about the community's beliefs. They came upon neighbors with queer beliefs every day, so such things were normal to them. Furthermore, the settlement was pious and quiet, and they would no more say a word against private piety than they would against God himself. But that this group of people lived in such an isolated fashion, so independent and unsociable, enraged them. The settlement seemed to be growing richer with each season and all that the townspeople wanted from it was some honest money every now and then, but since they were never able to sell it much of anything—on the contrary, they kept buying from it—they came to regard it as the one useless village in all creation. In the autumn they still brought their corn to be ground in the community mill, because by now the community could afford to grind it for less than any other mill thereabouts, but after the snows had come and drifts blockaded the mountain passes they no longer broke into the valley to see if their neighbors needed help, and in spring they drove their wagons along the crest of the valley and peered down at the neatly shingled roof tops and the black fields and the clouds of white apple blossoms, and they spat.

But even as the community flourished it began to wither. The self-taught surveyors had long since staked out the cemetery, and now every spring more of the elders were buried and fewer came to sing at graveside. In time, the meeting house had more than enough settees and chairs to go around. Every room in the dormitories had its bed and cabinet, and each door had smooth working hinges and a firm latch. The craftsmen had less and less work to do, and no need for apprentices. The townspeople bought fewer wrought-iron fixtures since other goods had come into household fashion: brass hinges, locks which could be concealed in a door frame, porcelain door knobs. Fewer people came to have their corn ground at the mill; in the outside towns they were eating their corn on the cob or feeding it to pigs, and they imported wheat flour for bread. Almost no one came to buy the graceful rocking chairs, they were no longer in style.

They no longer needed to farm as much land as formerly. Yet they allowed nothing to fall back into mere wilderness. They slashed at the edge of the woods whenever it tried to advance on the fields, and they sickled the fields clean of brambles. They kept the roads clear and the walks trim, and they reset whatever stone steps had been turned aside by frost or thaw. Each spring they scrubbed the walls and floors of the vacated rooms, and after a day-long airing they fastened the windows and shut the door on the coming year. All this came on so gradually that it seemed no fewer rooms were being lived in than before, but rather as if the empty rooms had been added secretly, one by one, and the buildings grew larger with each season.

One afternoon the last cabinetmaker died, leaving behind him in an empty carpentry shop a most delicately balanced, half-completed rocking chair which no one knew how to finish. They had become repairmen and grounds-keepers. Each thing was kept in neat readiness. The green lawns and silent mansions looked not abandoned but as if they were awaiting their rightful owner, some royal personage who might arrive at any moment to take up residence. The handful of people who tended the grounds and took care of the buildings gathered together in one dormitory. Whenever anyone needed anything he took a key from the trustee's office and walked along the deserted streets to this or that shop, unlocked the door on the echoing stillness, took whatever he needed, and locked the door after him when he left. Then these few also diminished. The arrival of a rightful owner did not take place. Some statute of limitations ran out. The village was sold—grounds, buildings, movables, and all—to become a school.

I arrived in the dead of winter. A bus left me on the highway, and I walked down a snow-lined road which curved through an empty wood out onto the school grounds. It was like walking onto the top of a white marble table. The road ran straight ahead across the level snow, passed between two long rows of buildings, and then halted abruptly just short of touching the gentle curve of the mountainside. On the left there was a steep rise, and on the right the school grounds went out flat and broke off in mid-air. The school was in winter recess; the walks were shoveled and the windows sparkled but all the doors were closed, the road was empty, and the fields were silent. A little ways on I came to what looked like some gray boards jammed upright in the snow beside the road. They were narrow slabs of stone, each one with a set of initials and a date cut into it, and taken all together they made up a small cemetery. There were a half-dozen or so of these stones in a cluster by the road, then the great stretch of snow in back of them ran out smooth and empty to the edge of the grounds where it sheared away. It was a scant graveyard for such a sizable community as had lived here, but since they had started with no belief in carving full names on headstones they probably had ended with no belief in putting up any headstones at all. The entire township lay sequestered here. They left no living behind but took all to the grave, for among the rules they lived by were those which said that men and women must not meet upon the fields, not touch hand to hand, not cohabit.

I walked into the empty village, looking for the administration building. The headmaster had written me that it had a school signboard hanging from a post outside the door, and that he would be waiting for me inside, in his office. Each of the buildings stood clear and alone on the smooth white snow; they were large, with flat walls of straight-edged stone or tight parallel clapboards, and the windows were lined up one above the other and one beside the other, with a grid of identical glass panes. They were spaced here and there, but always squared off from each other, so that the long lines of one never ran at an angle or tangent to another, but each made a firm parallel with each to the four corners of the horizon. The headmaster's building was set back from the road a bit further than the others. It was painted white, was three stories high and somewhat larger than most, and in the dead center of the building was a door which seemed to be made from a gray stone slab. Above it a sign said: HANDS TO WORK AND HEARTS TO GOD. Beneath the door were two millstones laid one upon the other, but with the top one pushed back, to make a pair of steps. The building seemed about to lose its body, to vanish into its outline. It was some trick of the view. The level snow and smooth white walls gave nothing for sight to catch hold of: the building went flat against the sky as if it were drawn on paper. They had done their work that well. They had hacked, slashed, burned, pulled, chopped, shoveled, and raked the land until it was as flat and clear as a draftsman's table. Then from some invisible bench mark all distances had been so measured, all angles so calculated, that even now I felt myself standing safe between invisible guidelines, as on a path in which each turn and step had been prepared. Here each thing was measured, cut true to its imagined shape—chiseled, filed, sanded—trimmed down until all which must not be was not, and only what was necessary for the end remained: the thing in itself, its own finality and end.

I gave in to all this. I felt a pure security, serenity, stillness. The raging inner man was dumfounded, silenced at last. My other self, all these months meditating at my side, now slid in close and with a whisper took my right arm and urged me down the path toward the door, to take the job.

After supper, after I had cleared the table and washed the dishes and swept the floor, I lay down on the bunk in the living room. Two women lived overhead, and one of them had just put on high heels and was hurrying back and forth. I was thinking about Sophia Alden, about her being more than thirty-five years old, and about her looks. As I said, she was not bad looking. After a while I heard a door slam, then the clack-clack of high heels coming down the stairway, the swish as the front door opened, crashed shut, then silence. I don't know how long I lay there. The apartment house was quiet now and you could hear the murmur of footsteps, or voices, or cars and taxis passing along the street, or water rushing in the pipes, little blurred noises. It was lonely, all right. I thought about Sophia Alden, about her being older than I was but not so much older, not too much older. I thought of other people I could visit but mostly I thought about Sophia. Anyway, I got up and took a bath and then hunted out her number in the phone book and telephoned her. Her hello was tentative and uncertain.

"Hello," I sang out. "This is Frank. I'm out taking a walk. Shall I stop by your place for coffee?"

"Frank. How wonderful! *Yes.*" Her voice cleared, came into focus. "Do come by. The apartment's a mess. I'll put a new pot of coffee on the stove right now."

I told her that I'd be right over. Then I hurried into some clothes, ran up to the Square, and hopped a cab to the corner of the street where she lived.

10

Sophia looked up at me from the open bed, her eyes glistening and uncertain. The mattress sank beneath my knee. I slid hurriedly down beside her, hiding the sight of us from each other. She was embarrassed now, ashamed at having invited me to her apartment and at having so quickly drawn me to the bed, humiliated by her seduction of me. She put her hands on my neck, smiled wretchedly, then jerked them away. I kissed her and tried to think of what to do to put her at ease. I kissed her once more, then drew her arms over her head and pressed them back into the pillow, clamping her wrists in my hand, nailing her to the bed. Sophia shuddered, went limp with pleasure. "What are you going to do to me?" she whispered.

"I don't know," I muttered, squeezing her wrists until they must hurt. "I haven't decided yet."

She let her eyes fall shut. "Torture me," she gasped.

I kissed her slack breast, kissed tenderly the bruised flesh where the discarded bra still left its imprint, then slyly turned my cheek and pressed close to listen—her heart was thudding wonderfully fast. She was going to have a good time if I was clever enough. I renewed my handcuff grip, stretched her out brutally, and began to kiss her throat. She stirred against me. "Be careful," I said, pulling away. But she languidly pushed her leg between mine—flank, thigh, belly. "Watch out," I cried, throwing myself over her. "Oh, God. Sophy!" After a while I slid off Sophia, rolled onto my back, then the bed lamp lighted up: I put an arm over my eyes.

"This hot-blooded youth," she said with sarcasm.

I didn't say anything; let her enjoy her little vengeance.

"Haste makes waste," she went on loudly.

I took my arm from my eyes. Sophia was on her hands and knees in the center of the dazzling bed, looking at me. Her eye make-up was bleary, and her lipstick was smeared all around so it looked as if I had punched her in the mouth.

"You still look quite beautiful," I told her. "For a woman your age, that is."

She studied my eyes, tried to discover if I were joking. "You snake," she said at last. "And don't laugh!"

"Come on," I said. "You're all right."

She looked discouraged. She padded to the bureau, glanced at herself in the tall mirror, then took up a brush and began yanking it through her hair. Sophy's hair was black—mostly black, that is, with little flecks of gray here and there—cut in short, crisp curls. She had a grand back with a deep spine, and a rear that was dented and dimpled with its own weight. Every time she jerked her arm the flesh on her buttocks shimmered in the lamp light. Sophy was not what you would call fat, but certainly she was comfortably spread. I watched it for a while.

"I'm hungry," I said.

She stopped brushing, looked at me in the mirror. "Hungry? How can you be hungry when you haven't *done* anything?"

"I'm still hungry." I stretched, folded my hands under my head, and laid myself out. "I want something to eat."

She was still looking at me in the mirror. She made a face, then set down her hairbrush, put on a pale coffee-colored robe, and swept into the kitchen. I got up and wrapped a towel around my waist. Her apartment was wide open and empty: the bed space was at this end, and at the other end there were a couple of chairs, a coffee table (our stained cups, the blackened TV), then a dim and empty dining area, and the lighted kitchen. She was staring moodily into the refrigerator. "What do you want?" she asked.

"What do you have?"

"Eggs? I could fry you some eggs," she suggested. "Cold chicken. Cold cuts. Cheese. Tomatoes. Celery. Milk. How about some eggs?" she said briskly.

I drew out the platter with the chicken and handed it to her. "White meat," I said. She set it on the counter, held the chicken steady with a fork while she began slicing. She cut off a long white oval rimmed with crusty gold skin. "How's the career?" I asked. Sophia was rather rich, but she worked in a library to keep busy.

"It's not exciting," she said flatly. "I'd like to quit, but I don't know what else I could do for a job." She sliced cautiously, delicately.

"What time do you have to be at work tomorrow?"

"At nine." Her voice was sharp. "And if you don't keep your hands out of this platter you're going to be missing a finger!"

"This is wonderful stuff. What shall we have to drink?" I took another piece of chicken.

"There's scotch, and some sherry, and a little gin. In the cabinet next to the refrigerator. I don't want a thing," she added.

I poured myself a glass of sherry, picked up a thin slab of chicken, and took them on a stroll around the dining area.

"If you'd only stay still a minute I'd give you a plate," she said, sounding harassed.

"How come you don't have any dining-room furniture?"

"Because I'm living on my salary. I've paid for everything in this apartment with my own money, the money I've earned. If I didn't work, people would call me a wealthy old bag." A muted appeal had crept into her voice. "They probably call me that, anyway."

"I'm glad I'm not that rich." I let myself belch loudly, then scooped up a few more slivers of white meat.

"Do you want any more?" She was looking prim now, but I doubted that she was honestly annoyed.

"No," I said, grabbing a chicken wing.

Sophia thrust the chicken into the refrigerator and glanced quickly around the kitchen to see that everything was in its proper place, pointedly ignoring me, then she snapped out the light and sailed briskly away. I took the bottle and glass into the bedroom, propped myself on the pillow at the head of the bed, and watched her in the bathroom washing away her make-up, her cosmetics. Ordinarily I'm not much of a slob, but it seemed to me that Sophia liked it. I nibbled on the chicken wing and kept an eye on her. "I haven't enjoyed myself so much in a hundred years," I told her. She continued her careful washing, as if she had barely heard me and did not care. "I haven't felt so good in five hundred years," I amended. "A thousand years, maybe." She did not even turn her head. I licked my fingers and took up the bottle. She had a handsome bathroom, certainly better than mine: lots of rosy tile, glittering faucets, a wet mirror, and a thick fleecy bath mat. Finally, Sophia completed her wash and came out, then I lay back while she wrapped a steaming towel over my face—ah, that was good—scrubbed my mouth and chin, wiped my fingers. That was her idea, actually. She held my hand and looked at me some moments. "You pig," she said tenderly. "How do you stay so thin when you eat so much?"

"Nerves," I explained. "I have these tense nerves."

She smiled. Her lips were washed pale, and you could see all the wrinkles around her eyes. She caught me looking at her. "I could never make it as a natural beauty," she said.

Sophia pulled open the top drawer of her bureau—it rattled with jars, pots, perfume bottles, brushes, combs, pearly beads, files and emery boards, hairpins, bracelets, eyebrow pencils, clips, scissors, curlers—then she sat beside me on the edge of the bed and faced the mirror. In profile, you could see how the flesh under her chin sagged ever so gently. She tied a bib around her neck, letting it hang down beneath her throat, sprinkled a few drops of something on her fingers and began to rub it onto her cheeks, her forehead, her chin. "You don't have to do that for me," I told her. She smiled thinly but continued to watch herself working in the mirror. She added color to her cheeks, then took a pencil and slowly sketched along her eyebrows. She filled a little brush with dark powder and began stroking it onto her eyelid. "Tell me some more about this older man that you haven't been seeing recently," I said.

"I've already told you all you need to know."

"Is he unmarried?"

"That's what he says." She paused a moment to study the eyelid in the mirror. "And I can believe it. He's *not* the impulsive type."

"Maybe something will come of it." I was beginning to feel uncomfortable, in the wrong.

"Yes," she said lightly. "There's always that remote possibility."

"Sophia, what the hell am I doing here?"

"Oh, don't start *that*." She turned on me: one eye was sensual, dark and heavy-lidded, the other was naked and old. "I haven't seen him recently because he's not seeing me. It's really quite simple." She watched me a moment longer with those weird eyes, then turned back to the mirror to complete her face.

"You're all right, Sophy. I like you."

"I like you too, Frank. And let's not get sentimental."

She finished making up her face, removed the bib, put on pearl earrings, and tied a black ribbon around her neck. Then she closed the bureau drawer and stood up to look at herself in the mirror, squaring her shoulders, tightening the sash around her pale-coffee-colored robe. Finally she turned, faced me, waited.

"You look grand," I said. "But why did you go to all this trouble?"

"For you," she said mildly. "So you could muss it up. Don't you want to muss me up?"

I turned off the bed lamp. The little lamp on the bureau gave a shadowy gold shine to her robe, made her face dim and serene. She stood quietly with her hands at her sides while I loosened her sash, spread the robe open about her throat, her shoulders. "Oh, you rat," Sophia whispered. "Kill me. Murder me."

I always liked a long walk home in the early morning, liked the freshness of the air and the empty streets, the growing light. The Charles River is gray as glass, and the city lies all becalmed and asleep. I do not know how long I had been sleeping when Sophia's snores woke me; it was a marvel she did not wake herself up, she was so noisy. I drifted back to sleep, then some while later I realized that I was awake again, so I crept out of bed, took my clothes into the bathroom, washed off, and dressed. Sophia had rolled onto her stomach in the middle of the bed and was sleeping quietly now. I gave her shoulder a pat and drew the covers over her. "Are you going?" she asked. I said yes. She kissed my hand and turned back to sleep. Sophia lived in a new apartment house, a cement box with an outside stairway that zigzagged down through three long balconies; when I looked back from the street I could not tell which set of windows belonged to her. It was pleasant to walk along, just looking at things. The air was gray and damp and chill. The grass was soaked and the sidewalk was covered with big wet yellow leaves, and it was so quiet you could hear when a drop of water fell off a branch onto the street. All the houses had the shades down and the windows were filled with black, as if it were still night inside. Massachusetts Avenue was empty and wide-looking, and you could see all the way up to Cambridge Common where the trees looked delicate as cobwebs. When I was walking through the Common the lamps went out, glowing yellow for a moment as they cooled. Now the sky was pale and milky. The Square was quiet. There were some taxis parked here and there by the curb, and an empty bus at the subway kiosk. The light touched the buildings along the top, touched the weathered sandstone capitals and scrolled corbels, made the familiar structures look like unsuspected monuments revealed for the first time by a receding tide. I walked on to my apartment house. A flock of sparrows fluttered down and went hopping around in the middle of the street, eager for breakfast. I thought about Sophia—I hoped that she was going to have a happy life—but mostly I just walked along looking at things. It was always lovely to walk home in the early morning like that, it was the best part.

11

My wife is pregnant. She has no morning sickness, but in the evening she has prepared a sizzling dinner, steaming and running with juices, set the loaded plates upon the table, and then looked at her food and said she was not hungry after all. You would not guess that she was pregnant, to look at her. She goes to work each morning at nine, comes home to make lunch, then goes back to work for the afternoon. Only in the evening she grows languorous and soon drops into a warm slumber. So I have these late hours to myself, to sit and listen to the wind rattling the dry leaves or to walk across the hall for a cup of coffee with the neighbors. The house is one hundred and some years old and they say it has been moved here and there about the hills. Now the frost has started her again, has swung the doors on their hinges, twisted nails around in their sockets, and set the timbers creaking like a schooner. If I place a tennis ball on the floor it will escape into the next room, rolling under the desk and around the chair and over the threshold. There is a fireplace in every room, and the bathtub crouches on claw feet beneath the stairway to the upper floors. It's a big old house and lots of people have lived in it. In this mournful wind the steeple clock striking the hour sounds like a bell buoy. Everyone is asleep. Only the child, curled around its miniature face and no longer than the end of my thumb, is busy at his long dream.

12

One noon I went up to the Square and saw a girl so beautiful that my heart began knocking wildly in my chest. *God, I thought, that's the one I want.* She waited on the curb—her black coat blown open, her sky-blue sweater, and sea-green skirt—as lonesome as a mermaid in the middle of the sea. I turned and walked blinded down Brattle Street. Then I ran back, but she was gone and I was lost.

The next day it was raining, the thin slant lines almost invisible on the gray air. At noon I buttoned up my raincoat and went in close along the store fronts, under an awning and under the brim of somebody's umbrella, until I reached the Square. I joined a group which had gathered just inside the portico of the Coop and posted myself beside one of the columns. A man in a canvas rain hat went past, a girl with a rosy umbrella, a couple of women in kerchiefs of thin gray plastic, a young man with leather elbow patches and a big black umbrella, a girl with a long wet braid, a man holding a folded newspaper over his head. I don't know how long I kept watch, but she was not across at the subway and she did not come by. The rain was falling heavily now, rushing. A cold mist edged into the portico and people began to stir uneasily. A bearded man in a glistening black poncho joined us between the columns, a young couple holding hands ran by, then the sidewalk was empty. People were standing in doorways, under the bank marquee, inside the glass foyer of the cafeteria, huddled beneath the eaves of the kiosk, beneath the wooden awning in front of the newspaper stand. Cars moved along cautiously, their head lamps sparkling white. Then little by little the air paled and brightened and the rain thinned. Traffic lights shimmered on the street. A student trotted across the Square, his jacket collar turned up about his neck, shoes splashing. People flowed onto the sidewalks again. The girl I had been waiting for ran past, bareheaded, clutching a book. I started after her. She hurried across the Square while I ran behind, wondering what to say if I caught up with her. Then she slipped farther, farther ahead and vanished in the crowd. I slowed down, stopped, but my heart went on banging in my chest and my head echoed. I pushed into Hazen's, bought a cup of coffee, and slumped down at one of the long tables by the window. I looked at the rain and across the avenue at the slate roofs and their branches above the wall in Harvard Yard. I was too tired to think about the girl or about loneliness or about anything. After a while I was calmed and the scattered pieces of my mind began to come back, one by one, like blackbirds returning to an empty tree. Susan Norse came along with an armful of books at her breast, her face turned from the rain, her eyes squinted. I waved, beckoning. She came in and slid her books wearily onto the table.

"How are you?" I asked.

"Wet," she said. She untied the knot at her throat and drew the damp silk kerchief from her head. She had smooth bronze hair, cut like a bell. I hung her coat on a hook and asked could I get her anything. She said that she had just finished lunch. "But I'd rather like some tea," she added vaguely. "With lemon." I went to the counter and returned with her tea and a bowl of soup for myself. Susan was pinching the lower edge of her hair with a paper napkin; her face was wan. "Thank you," she said. "How have you been?"

"Miserable."

"Oh dear." She looked troubled. "What's the matter?"

"I'm going crazy. There's a girl I want to meet. I've seen her a couple of times in the Square and I don't know her name. She's driving me out of my head."

Sue raised the lid of the little tin pot and peered inside, gently prodding the tea bag with a spoon. Then she put down the spoon and looked at me. "Do you know anything about her?"

"She's about your age and I think she's a student. You might even know her."

"What does she look like?"

"She's beautiful and has long dark hair."

She gazed blankly at the table a few moments, thinking. Then she closed the pot, held the lid with a finger, and carefully poured her cup of tea. She looked at me again. "A lot of my friends have long hair. Can you be a little more specific?"

"No."

"Black hair?"

"No, not *black*. Dark. It's very bright, actually. A very bright, dark color—this is insane."

She looked at me, waiting.

"Let's change the subject," I said.

She sipped her tea and said nothing. Susan was a pretty girl with wide blue eyes and glossy white skin. Last year she had been going around with a friend of mine, a painter named Nikos, only something had gone wrong and now she was studying for an M.A. in fine arts. Nikos had moved to the back of Beacon Hill and I had not seen him in months. Whenever Sue was happy or excited her face turned pink, but the breakup had left her looking like porcelain. We talked this way and that way about painting, but we never brought up his name. When she had finished her tea she lit a cigarette.

"I think I have mono," she said listlessly. "Mononucleosis."

"Mononucleosis?"

"Yes. Or a cold. I've had a sore throat for days."

"You shouldn't walk around in the rain."

"I know. I know." She sighed and smoked her cigarette and looked idly at the other tables; they were mostly empty now.

"Maybe you would know this girl if you saw her," I suggested. "You might know her name, at least."

"I don't know everybody."

"Look, are you doing anything tomorrow, at noon?"

"I have classes. And things." Her voice was tentative. "Why?"

"Never mind. Forget it. The whole thing is crazy. Forget it."

"I'd be glad to help," she said languidly.

"I have to get back to work," I said.

She shrugged. I held her books while she tied the kerchief over her head, then we stood in the doorway and looked at the rain. "Well, good luck anyway," she said. Then Susan crossed to the Yard and I headed back to the office.

The next day at noon I went to the Square and stood by one of the columns in front of the Coop and kept watch on the people going past. Little by little the cold began to soak in. I buttoned my raincoat, turned up the collar, and put my hands in my pockets. Everyone was walking hunched up. I stamped my feet for a while, then crossed to the center and strolled around the subway kiosk. I read the headlines at the newspaper stand, blew on my fingers, stamped my feet. Then I crossed back and strolled slowly around the Square. The sky was hazy gray and the sun was pale. I walked down the avenue to Hazen's. I opened the door—crashed into her —staggered inside as she went out. The place was crowded and Sue Norse was standing at the counter.

"Hello," she said hoarsely. "Have you had lunch?"

"Did you see the girl who just went out of here?"

"No." She picked up her tray with its teapot and cup. "Why?"

"I want to know her name. She's the one I told you about yesterday."

"She just went out?"

"Just when I came in."

"Maybe it was Nancy." She looked doubtful. "I just had lunch with her. Why don't you come and sit down," she added hoarsely.

I followed Susan to a place by the wall and sat down opposite her. She set the cup and little teapot on the table, then slowly loaded the tray with sloppy dishes, crumpled paper napkins, cups, glasses, and shoved it aside. Her eyes were watery and her nose was red, chafed.

"How do I know we mean the same girl?" I asked her.

"I roomed with her two summers ago in New York. She has very long hair."

"Lots of your friends have very long hair."

"Her name is Nancy White. She's a student, a senior." She studied me a moment. "Do you want me to introduce you?"

"*No!*"

"Well, you needn't snarl at me." She looked full at me with her sulky watery eyes. "I'm only trying to be helpful. You were so eager to meet her." She took a paper napkin and began blowing her nose, then paused and looked at me again. "Do you want her phone number?"

"No. But thanks anyway," I added.

The crowd at the counter had dispersed somewhat, so I went for a cup of coffee. When I returned Susan was gazing sleepily into the teapot, idly probing the tea bag with her spoon.

"You sound like you have a bad cold," I told her. "Why don't you go home and go to bed?"

"I *am* going home."

"Have you been to a doctor?"

"I haven't got a temperature." Her voice was husky. "Every couple of hours I drink a spoonful of TH and C. It has codeine in it. It's rather marvelous stuff. Every time you buy a bottle the little man at the drugstore writes your name in a book. I feel like an addict already."

"How can I be sure we have the same girl in mind?"

"Nancy is a lovely girl."

"The name sounds phony."

"Really, Frank. You amaze me." She filled her cup with tea, then squeezed the lemon over it and watched the drops bleach the dark color away.

"What's her phone number?" I asked.

I telephoned Nancy White that evening, told her my name, told her that I had seen her in the Square and that Sue Norse had given me her phone number. Then I asked her if she would meet me sometime for a coffee. She said yes. I asked her could she meet me in front of the Coop tomorrow at noon. "Yes," she said. "But how will I recognize you?"

"I'll see you first. I'll know you."

"I hope so," she said.

So when I saw her coming across the Square I stepped forward and waved, then she saw me and we met on the curb. People were walking around us. "I've seen you three times and I spoke to you last night," I said.

She smiled. "Then you must be the one I'm looking for."

13

The next day was Saturday. We met in the afternoon and went for a slow walk by the river, walked on the wide bank, walked up and down beneath the empty sycamore trees, talking. The sky grew white and the sun faded. We stopped for a moment to look at the water. "Are you cold?" I asked her.

"Yes. A little. But you must be freezing in that raincoat."

"Let's walk back to the Square."

We turned and headed toward Boylston Street. I thought about suggesting that we walk to my apartment, then pushed it out of my mind to think about later. We did not speak for a while and it was wonderful to be able to walk together, seeing the same things and not talking.

"Where do you come from?" I asked.

"I was born here, right here in Cambridge. And you?"

"I was born in Boston."

"Then we moved to Exeter in New Hampshire and then to Concord, Mass. What about you?"

We talked about our families and where we had lived. Nancy's mother's name was Margaret, her father's name was John, and she had a brother twelve years older whose name was also John. Her father was headmaster of a coeducational private school in Concord; before that he had taught at Exeter, before that he had been a student at Harvard and before that he had grown up on Kirkland Street in Cambridge. Her father's father had been a lawyer, and that father's father had been a doctor and a friend of William James, the psychologist. "My grandmother liked to say we were related to Peregrine White. And you know who *he* was."

"No. Tell me."

"He was the first child of the Pilgrims and he planted an apple tree in Marshfield." Nancy laughed

We had stopped outside the Gabrielle. "Shall we go in for a cup of coffee?" I asked.

"Yes, let's. I'm turning to ice."

We went down the brick steps. A rusted café table was chained to the bottom of the stair rail and a drift of stiff brown leaves lay in the corner by the door. Inside the air was warm, fragrant with pastry and coffee and cocoa. Madeleine was behind the counter, arranging cakes inside a paper box. She smiled, tied up the box, and briskly set it aside. I asked for two American coffees. It was a tiny shop; the walls were whitewashed stone, the little tables were bright red, blue, green, yellow. The red parasol for the outdoor table was furled in the corner. I asked Nancy did she want any pastry.

"Are you going to have some?" she answered, cautious.

"Sure."

"I guess I'll have the same," she said.

"Why don't you pick out a table," I suggested. "I'll bring this over."

It felt good to sit down and get warm. Nancy opened her coat, unfolding it back over the chair. She was wearing a black sweater with a V-neck and no blouse; she looked very happy. I wanted to go on talking, but it was awkward because anyone could overhear us. Madeleine turned on the lights in the window, glanced up at the sidewalk, then began energetically wiping the top of the glass counter. In the near corner a bald-headed man was sipping tea, reading a newspaper, and a boy in short pants was seated at the table next to the bakery room, silently loading a toy dump truck with sugar cubes. We murmured our conversation. Suddenly five girls tumbled in, chattering and laughing, filling the room. They draped their coats over the chairs near us, heaped their books on the floor, took tea and exotic pastries, and settled at last around the table beneath the front window. Nancy had been watching them with mild curiosity, now she turned to me. "I was never that young," she said.

"How old are you?"

"Twenty-one, going on twenty-two." She smiled.

"I'm twenty-eight."

"That's good."

"And unmarried and so forth," I added.

"I had hoped as much. I was brought up rather strictly." She laughed uneasily and pushed back her sleeves; her arms were white, covered with dark golden down.

"Are you going with someone? Are you engaged?" I asked.

She looked at me a moment. "I'm not engaged."

"You are going with someone, more or less." My insides felt very light, like I was jumping from a cliff.

She hesitated. "Well. No. No, I'm not going with anyone. I'm not engaged to be married."

"I've been honest with you."

"I know." She looked troubled. She started to lean back, then sat up. "I—I'm not engaged and I'm not going around with anyone here, but I have a friend who lives in New York. We write letters," she added.

"I don't want to make a fool of myself." It was not an endearing trait, but she seemed not to notice.

"I was almost engaged to him. We were very close, close to each other. But we aren't so close any more." She glanced at the table, adjusted her cup in its saucer, then looked at me.

"Let's forget it." My insides floated back together. "We can always talk about it later if we want to."

"He doesn't really write letters, only notes. He cuts things out of magazines, articles, or sometimes a comic strip from a newspaper, and mails them to me with a note. Sometimes he sends one of those funny greeting cards, the kind with a little joke printed inside."

I wanted to say he sounded like a nut, but I didn't say anything.

"He sounds strange. But he isn't. He just doesn't have anything to say to me, that's all."

She smiled somewhat and I smiled back. We had finished our coffee, but neither of us seemed ready to leave. I felt exhausted. We looked at the schoolgirls and at the boy in short pants who was trying to build an igloo with the sugar cubes. A young couple came in and a moment later they were followed by three fat women, each carrying an armful of bundles. The place was getting crowded, so we put on our coats and continued our walk. By the time we reached the Square the sky had turned ashen. I asked Nancy if she could stop in at my apartment. "Sure," she said. She looked very happy.

The apartment building had been put up about seventy-five years ago, and it looked like a red brick fortress. The foyer was elegant, paved in worn octagonal tile, but the flats inside had been so badly cut up that some were like closets and others were like public meeting halls. I had one of the big ones, a gallery. I unlocked the door and pulled on the overhead light and you could see all my rooms at once. "This is all there is," I told her. It was so cold that I could see my breath; I tried to speak more gently. "And the bathroom has a toilet that works when you pull a chain."

"Oh, it's very nice," she said politely, looking at me.

"They won't let me paint the walls. If I could paint them a lighter color it would look better." She needed cheering up.

"It's not so bad," she assured me. Nancy looked sadly at the dim windows and the cinder courtyard outside, then her gaze drifted to the doorway and the steamer trunk with the telephone on it, then to the canvas sling chair and the cot and the rigid chair of black oak, to the floor boards veneered with deck paint, the little patch of rug, the ornate radiator scrolled with cast-iron grape leaves, the long gray string from the bulb overhead, the huge mirror in its gilded rococo frame, the wall hung with my pornographic paintings. She was disappointed, all right.

"Well, it's cheap and it's easy to keep clean," I told her. My voice boomed and echoed; I had forgotten how the big room echoed.

"It's very neat. And it certainly is clean."

"I washed the floors this morning. I do it every Saturday. I just slosh soap and water around, swab it around, and then mop it. Most of the water pours between the floor boards into the cellar, but nobody cares. The trash barrels are down there." I was beginning to sound desperately foolish. "Do you think it's gloomy?"

"No." She looked startled, surprised. "Not at all."

I pulled the shades down and drew the drapes shut, then turned on the lamp. "Is this better?"

"It's fine. I like it." She smiled.

"It's a big room—maybe it's too big—but that's what I like about it."

"It's perfect," she announced, strolling over to the wall to take a look at the paintings.

14

When I was a small child my father taught me how to count and how to write numerals. Then one day I discovered that if I made a three and turned it around it was not a line any more but the picture of a bird, a sea gull. It was wonderful. After that I tried again and again to make pictures of other things, but it was too hard. If I scribbled enough lines I could sometimes find a picture in them, but that was not as good as drawing what I wanted. It was like when I was eating a slice of bread I could stop after a few bites, look at it, and sometimes I could make out a duck or a fish. My father showed me how to draw a face in a circle. The faces didn't have bodies, so I learned to make a line across the bottom of the face and then add the lines slanting down from the middle. One day a friend of mine named Jack told me that I was drawing people wrong because I had left out the bodies. I drew another face with arms and legs, looked at it, and I could not discover anything wrong or missing. Then Jack drew a picture and instead of putting the arms along under the face he made a line straight down from the chin, then he put the arms across it at the top and added the legs at the bottom. I was astounded. After that I was able to draw people just as well as stars, flowers, flying sea gulls, and waves. Jack and I used to lie on our stomachs on the floor with crayons and paper and think of something out loud—say an airplane, or a steamboat, or something—then we would draw it and compare pictures. One afternoon we decided to draw a house. I had never thought about a house so I began looking around at the walls and tried to draw the wall with the window, the shade, and the curtains, but it was too hard. Jack drew the outside of a house. At first it was a square with a pointed top, but after he put in the door and the window you could see that it was the front of a house. Houses soon became easy to draw. I made whole streets and towns on one page, the chimneys with smoke curling out in loops. Later my father showed me perspective. He drew me a picture of our house and added lines to the roof and the middle and the bottom; when he connected the lines—it was magical—you could see the house from the corner. When I began going to school there were many things to learn how to do and we did not have much time for drawing. One morning the teacher showed us how to weave a mat from strips of colored paper, then she came around with the paper and let each of us choose two different colors. It was odd how if you put some colors side by side nothing happened, but when you touched two other colors together they seemed to light up. It was fun to draw with colors, but it was only a sort of play for children. In class you had to be smart, had to learn different things, and had to remember, then at recess you had to be pushy and quick. In the afternoon when school was out there were lots of things to do, friends to play with, games and sports. Sometimes when it was raining and I was alone indoors I would draw things, but not very often. I could draw better than anyone in my grade at school—it was easy for me—but no one cared and it was not important anyway.

One afternoon I came in and asked my mother if I was an American. "Of course you are," she said. I told her that the boys at the playground had said I was an Italian and had tried to call me names again. "What names?" she asked, looking at me suspiciously.

"They called me a wop and a guinea." I burst into tears and my mother pulled my head into her lap, hugged me, patted me.

"Shush, shush, shush. What are you crying about? Remember Christopher Columbus discovered the whole new world. Remember? Christopher Columbus discovered America and he was Italian," she whispered. "And Amerigo Vespucci—they named America after him—he was Italian." She fell silent and went on stroking my head. "John Cabot—he was really Giovanni Caboto—he discovered North America and he was Italian."

"The Pilgrims discovered North America," I told her resentfully. "They landed at Plymouth Rock."

"Use your handkerchief."

I wiped my eyes and nose.

"The greatest artists in the world are Italians," she went on quietly. "Dante, Leonardo da Vinci, Michelangelo, Botticelli, Benvenuto Cellini, Puccini, Verdi, Caruso, Toscanini—" She peeped into my eyes to see if I was feeling better. "All Italians."

"Who cares about Dante, anyway?"

"Who called you those names?"

"Danny Creegan."

"Don't play with him any more," she said firmly.

"But he's my *friend*."

"Well, the next time he starts to call you names, you tell him he's a mick. Tell him he's an Irish mick."

My mother's words shocked me; whenever people called you names you were supposed to shout, *Sticks and stones may break my bones but names will never hurt me.* "If we're not Italian why should I care about Dante?"

"La lingua di Dante è la lingua di Paradiso. Do you know what that means? In heaven the angels speak Italian." My mother went

on and on about how the very greatest artists were always Italians. "Only Michelangelo could paint a picture of God," she said. But I had heard these stories before. I wanted to go back to the playground, wanted to try calling Danny Creegan a mick, so I was relieved when at last my mother told me to wash my face and go.

We had many Caruso recordings, small brittle disks with a song on each side. My mother said that Enrico Caruso was a great artist. All the poor people who did not have enough money to buy a seat in the opera house used to wait outside and when Caruso was through the opera he would come to the window and sing all his arias over again, for free. She said that Caruso had a powerful voice which could reach from the stage to the last row of the highest balcony, but on the disks the music was small and the singing came from far away, as if we were listening to a toy orchestra. I did not care for Dante Alighieri; the end of his nose was bent so it almost touched his chin, and his mouth was bitter. We had several copies of *La Divina Commedia.* One was a big flat volume with heavy leaves of grayish paper and opposite each page there was an illustration, an engraving by Gustave Doré. It was interesting to discover what Hell and Purgatory and Heaven looked like, and when I peered closely I could see how all the little lines were curved and spaced to make the engraving. In Heaven and Purgatory everyone wore white robes, but in Hell they were naked. I wanted to linger over the naked people in Hell but the scenes were too dreadful—a woman had turned into a huge spider and a man was frozen up to his neck in ice, gnawing on the bald head of another man. Robinson Crusoe was my favorite story. It was a tall thin book with soft paper, bold print, and pen-and-ink sketches. The illustrations did not have borders around them: the story simply paused, there was a white space with the drawing in it, then the story continued. One of the first pictures showed Robinson Crusoe standing alone on a raft. I could not make out his face, but his head was bent and I knew that he was dejected. In back of him lay the messy scrawl of a wrecked ship and the fragile line of the horizon, and at his feet, a little curve of beach. The whole scene floated in empty space. I strengthened the frail lines of the sketch with a dark pencil, drew a sailboat on the horizon, then housed his lonely world inside a broad square frame. I liked Michelangelo Buonarroti. When he was carving the statue of David the Pope came along and said, "That's very good but—you know—I think the nose is a little bit too long." So Michelangelo filled a handkerchief with some marble chips and climbed up the statue and pretended to chisel off the end of the nose, then he dusted it with the handkerchief and when the bits of marble dribbled down the Pope said, "There, that's perfect." When Michelangelo finished the statue of Moses he stepped back to look at it, and it looked so real that he took his mallet and knocked Moses on the knee and said, "Speak!" If you go inside Saint Peter's Cathedral you can walk up to the statue and find where the chip is gone from the knee. In the end Michelangelo was old and sick, so they loaded his bed onto a big wagon and he journeyed back to his home town. He arrived at night and the gate to the town was too small for the wagon to go through, but all the people ran out and tore down the wall so that he could come inside.

Then one Christmas my father gave my mother a book of paintings. It was bound in black cloth, stamped with gold letters, and when you turned the pages they made a muffled rattle sound and gave out a clean odor. There were pictures of everything: God, Adam and Eve, the Crucifixion, Mary and Joseph, the Annunciation, Venus, Mona Lisa, parades on horseback, ceremonies with women in airy robes, returns and departures, portraits, tiled interiors, brawls, distances, clouds, flowers, girls bathing, storms, landscapes. Mostly I liked the crowd scenes, the battles and fantastic processions. I was careful not to gaze at the nude women any longer than at the other pictures—that would have been improper —but sometimes after a passing glance I would skip back a ways, then slowly turn the pages until I came to them for a second look. The women had smooth sumptuous bodies that looked massive but were weightless, like bodies in a dream. In a shadowy grove three women rested on tiptoe, musing together in the mild gaze of a young man; in other scenes they drifted overhead, their huge hips cushioned in cloudy gauze, or they bathed in torpid pools, broke languidly from an old man's embrace, and against the sky there was one whose breasts rained stars. The naked bodies fascinated and antagonized me: they seemed about to reveal so much yet they remained covered, withdrawn, and private. Venus stood on a floating scallop shell, wrapped in the scarf of her long gold hair. Her body was unshaded and easy to see, but her eyes were remote with a daydream of the pale water at her feet or the light figures who hovered about her. In another painting she lay at the edge of an open field; her body rested as gently as a willow leaf and it glowed like the sky, but her face was closed in sleep. At first I thought it was the turned flank or the billowing cloth that hid the secret, but it was not so. For one morning I opened the door and walked into the bathroom as my mother was rising from her bath —and we stood looking at each other—the water running from her shoulders, from her dark breasts, her soft stomach, streaming hair, thighs—then I turned and walked out. So I had seen all there was to see. Once I had wanted to create things and when I was a child I made a snake out of clay and blew into its mouth to see if it would come alive. Now I was no longer trying to compete with God. All I wanted was to uncover what God had made, wanted to see it clearly and to show it. The only time I felt wholly myself was when I was painting. I suppose that in the lonesome hours of sleep I was myself, and in the last letting go when making love, but only painting brought these far ends together. What was hidden in the beginning was still hidden and might remain closed forever. The naked body of a woman was only the shape within which it was concealed: you could penetrate it or devour it, but never lay it bare. The Venus who stood on the fluted waves drew a long coil of hair about her waist, but even if it had unbraided and slipped from her hand she would have remained as secret as that other one who lay asleep. It rested deep inside, and you had to know a lot about women, and you had to do a lot of painting before you could begin to show it.

15

Comes now Nancy White, dressed in a tight skirt and a wan blouse with a high collar and lace cuffs. I sat on my iron cot, watching her. She took her cup of coffee and walked slowly up and down the room, looking at the blazing light bulbs and the blue walls and at the furniture, pressing again the floor board where it creaked, returning at last to sit on the straight black oak chair. She glanced around for a table on which to leave her cup, then carefully set it on the floor.

"There's something we ought to talk about," I said.

"Well, I hope it works. Lately whenever I talk to anyone I wind up knowing less than when I started."

"Maybe you've been talking to the wrong people."

"Do you think anyone can really understand anyone else?" she asked.

"Yes."

"It hasn't worked that way for me." She sat up straight and crossed her legs, sliding one knee over the other. "Well, what do you want to talk about?"

The testimony was as follows:

"About this other person in New York," I said.

"What about him?"

"You're no longer close to him, you said."

She almost smiled. "That's the truth."

"When was the last time you saw him?" I asked.

"The last time I saw him was in August, the end of the summer."

"You haven't seen him since then."

"I haven't seen him at all since then."

"But you still write to each other," I said.

"He writes to me and I write back."

"You haven't broken off."

"What do you mean?" The defendant looked startled, baffled.

"I mean, he writes to you and you write to him."

"Yes. But that's all there is now." She colored slightly.

"Well, would you say it was finished between you two?"

She paused. "I'd say it was finishing."

Here the prosecuting attorney became quite severe: "How long does it take something like that to end?"

"I don't know. This is the first time I ever. I don't know. It wasn't supposed to end. I never thought about it ending."

"It was that bad?"

"Bad?" She took a long breath, then sighed. "Yes."

"Well, why don't you stop it? Break off."

"You think I should." She looked at me, so calm.

"It would make me happier," I said.

"I suppose it would make me happier too."

"To tell the truth, it would make me happy if you never thought of him again."

"I think I'd like that too." She smiled ruefully.

"Is it settled then?"

"Everything is happening so fast." She shut her eyes.

"Do you want me to go slower?"

She shook her head. "No," she said, opening her eyes. She uncrossed her legs, pressed her hands to her knees, and lowered her head. For a while she seemed to study her starched cuffs, the tiny ivory buttons. "I just wish I had finished it all a long time ago," she murmured.

"When did you meet him, anyway?"

"A couple of years ago," she said.

"You've known each other a long time. Where did you meet him?"

"Here in Cambridge. I met him when he was in his last year at the Business School. He works in Manhattan now, for International Business Machines. He does a lot of their thinking for them," she added. "He's good at that."

"Where were you last August?"

"He rented a beach house on the Cape. We went there." She looked at me.

"Oh? For how long?"

"Two weeks," she answered.

"Two weeks!" The prosecutor was thrown way off stride.

"It would have been better if we had—if I had—stopped seeing him. It was almost finished between us. But I didn't want to let it go, I didn't want it to end." She hesitated. "Do you want to hear this?"

"Yes."

"I didn't want it to end. Because if it ended, it would mean I had used myself up on something that was really nothing. If it ended, I had been wrong, terribly wrong. Do you understand? If it was all finished then I was finished too. Do you understand?"

"Yes."

Abruptly she stood up and went away, walked to the steamer trunk on which she had set her books and her purse. She lit a cigarette, then came back, dropped the burnt match into the saucer, and sat on the edge of the chair. "We had one of those cabins in Wellfleet. It had a bedroom and a tiny little bathroom and a tiny kitchen and a deck facing the bay. It was supposed to be like playing house—" She looked at me. "Do you want to listen to this?"

I said yes. It was like picking splinters out of my heart, but I listened. She told me about those two weeks—she quit after ten days, actually—and they were bad. She told me his name. He was one of those suffering bastards: suffering was his hobby, his art form, his career. He had certain noble qualities which I did not possess, such as believing that each of us is in some way responsible for the evil in the world, that we all have a share in the guilt. And he was so honest. He made sure that Nancy understood how very much he liked her but did not love her. He wanted to be certain that she knew what she was doing. He did not want to take advantage of her, he said. He was always saying that. Nancy finally finished the story, then got up and fetched herself another cigarette.

"I've known you a week," she said.

I didn't say anything. I had started to remember the Cape and had been overtaken with weariness.

"What are you thinking?" she asked softly.

"I'm not thinking, I'm just tired."

"Tired of?"

"Tired of affairs. Of my affairs, of other people's affairs."

Nancy didn't say anything. She bent down and crushed her cigarette into the saucer, rattling the cup and spoon, then she sat up and pushed back her hair and watched me with no smile. The room had grown silent.

I stood and took her wrist, turning back the lace cuff, trying to do it gently. "You're an old-fashioned girl."

She looked up at me a long moment. "An old-fashioned, wayward girl," she said quietly.

"Your hand is so cold."

"Is it?" Her voice had dwindled to a whisper. "Yes. I guess it is."

I cupped her fingers in my hands and blew on them, breathed on them, while she watched me with that calm gaze. Then I pulled her slowly to her feet and kissed her. Her eyes closed and she wavered, started to fall, recovered.

"What's wrong?" I asked her. "Are you all right?"

"Yes. I just— It must have been from standing so suddenly."

"Your hands are like ice. Are you all right?"

She smiled slightly. "I think I'm frightened."

"Don't be."

"Aren't you, at all?"

"Yes," I said.

16

Late one night, a loud banging at my door, and it was Dominick Saltares. He stood tentatively in the doorway, dressed in a thin ski jacket and pale summer trousers, his eyes shining from the cold. "Come out and have a drink." His chest was heaving, he seemed out of breath.

"Come in. Come in."

He stepped briskly into the apartment and halted. "Come on out. Have a drink." He smelled of beer and his forehead glistened. "You need a drink," he added.

"I don't want a drink," I said. "Come in and sit down."

"Come on, Annunzio!" He whirled angrily, grabbed my raincoat from the hook, and pushed it at my chest. "We haven't got all night. The bars are closing. Now put on your filthy coat and come out for a drink."

"What's up?" I put the raincoat back on the hook. I was tired. "Come in and sit down."

He looked baffled. "Aren't you coming with me? It's only a little way. It won't take long." He was still out of breath. "Are you coming? Or not?"

We stood eying each other. I did not want to go out, but his

face was slick with sweat and he looked awful. "All right," I said.
"If that's what you want."

I put on my overcoat and we headed up Mount Auburn Street.
Dom was hefty and had a lot of shaggy black hair. He was no
taller than I, but he was heavier, and when he was moving fast and
talking he created the impression of such great force that you forgot his size. I had never seen him drunk and he was not really
drunk now; or you might say that he was always drunk inside and
the little alcohol he took merely opened him up. He didn't say
much on the way to the bar. We pushed through the swinging
doors, then I settled into a booth while he hurried along the aisle
looking for a waitress. Some couples were already leaving. Dom
returned, pulled his ski jacket over his head, tossed it on the bench,
sat down. The waitresses in there had black dresses with white
aprons and we got one who wore rimless spectacles.

"Last call," she said. "What do you want?"

"Last call!" Dom cried. "We just *got* here."

She looked at him sourly. "Last call. Do you want anything?"

I asked for a glass of beer; Dom ordered four bottles for himself.

"You haven't got time for four bottles," the waitress told him.
"We close at midnight."

"All right," he said quickly. "Make it three bottles."

"You have to drink them here," she went on. "You can't take
them outside when you go."

"Please!" Dom said. "I know all that. I'll drink them here.
Please, just get the beer. Please."

The waitress regarded him skeptically, then walked away. Dom
threw himself back into the corner of the booth, closed his eyes,
collapsed. Cronin's was a big long room with three aisles and a bar
at the far end; a pair of crossed racing oars hung over the bar and
the back wall was decorated with dim brown photos of old football
and soccer teams. I had forgotten how noisy the place was. Dom
was still slumped in the corner, his face pale and damp.

"Are you falling asleep?"

The eyes opened blankly, then slowly focused. He put his fingers on the edge of the table and began to sit up. His lips turned white.

"You look sick," I said.

"No." His color returned somewhat and he pulled himself up. "I'm all right."

"What happened to you? What's the story?"

"The story is—" He leaned forward to look at me, looked at my eyes. "The story is, this afternoon I fucked this sweet young girl and this evening I made out with her mother."

That was Dominick. He was still waiting for me to say something. "I almost believe you," I said.

"It's the truth, the truth!" He slapped the table and laughed. "Do you think I'd lie? Do you think I dragged you in here to tell you lies?"

"Yes."

"No. It's God's awful truth." He laughed happily. "This afternoon I fucked this girl, this school girl, then tonight her mother came around to scare me off and I made it with her, too." He looked at me, expectant.

"Well?"

"Is that all you can say? I tell you I had this sweet downy pussy and her hairy mother. Understand? I had them both in one day, mother and daughter. I tell you I've just done what every young man dreams of doing, and all you can say is *well*?"

The waitress with the rimless spectacles returned carrying a tray: a glass of beer for me, two bottles for Dominick. He didn't say anything. The waitress set an empty glass in front of Dom, filled it, then set down the bottle and another opened bottle. "If you finish that before closing time you can order some more," she told him. She picked up the money and left.

"She should have been mother superior for some hospital," Dom said. "Did you see the way she carried the tray? Like it was some shit-full bedpan."

"What about Gretta?" Gretta Anders was that tall girl with ashen hair who belonged to him, more or less.

"What about her?" He looked mildly surprised; it was a fake look.

"Where does she fit into the picture?"

"She doesn't fit in at all," he said crisply. "She's out of it."

"I take it she's not living with you any more."

"I moved out about a month ago. She's still living in my old place. I'm living on the back side of Beacon Hill now. You'd know all this if you came around once in a while. You've been awful busy lately." He was irritated. "I don't want to talk about her."

So we drank our beer and did not talk for a time.

"Who is the new girl?" I asked.

"No one you know." He was still sore at me. "She's high class but stupid. The family lives somewhere off Brattle Street. Listen, I asked her once about her parents. She said, Daddy runs air lines and Mummy runs unsuccessful marriages." He smiled.

"She doesn't sound so stupid."

"Well, she is. I met her last summer when I was teaching at the cram school. She was one of my students. She's rich and good-looking and she's picked up a lot of phony sophistication from her chic friends, but she's not very bright. She goes to the something something Country Day School. It's expensive, whatever it is."

"How old is she?"

"Don't ask. She's got these little round breasts, you know? Just enough to hold in your hand."

"What happens if you get caught?"

"I didn't go looking for it. I'm not that way. She saw me one afternoon in a coffee house a couple of weeks ago and came over and sat down." He looked apologetic. "Said she needed some help with her Spanish."

"A real sophisticated approach."

"Then we went to my apartment. Don't laugh, don't laugh! Some girls are fascinated with the way I live. Some girls love shit.

Anyway, she asked if she could study there in the afternoons."

"Then she seduced you."

He looked at my eyes, then glanced away. "She drove me out of my mind," he croaked. He leaned forward, watching me. "She always sat on this flat sofa with her knees pulled up under her chin, reading. Then little by little she would slip down so I could see up her legs and listen to her underpants rubbing against the inside of her skirt. I was going out of my mind, Annunzio."

The music broke off, the bar vanished into shadow, everything lay stilled. They had turned off most of the lights and the air looked gray now; a few people stood in the aisles, slowly putting on coats, their voices lowered. Dom had tilted his head back and was draining his glass, his throat swallowing and swallowing and swallowing. He banged the empty glass down and glanced around, panting. There was still some beer left in one of the bottles; he wrapped his ski jacket around the bottle and tucked it under his arm. "Let's go," he said. Outside the air was cold and sweet, and I felt like washing my face in it. Dom was going on about the girl's mother.

"She said I was corrupting her daughter. I laughed in her face. Listen, I told her, before I met your daughter I thought all little girls were virgins. Your little girl has been very busy the past year." Dom brooded a moment, then went on. "You should have seen her. She stood there, shaking all over and calling me names. Said I was disgusting. I said I was disgusted with her hot-pants daughter."

Dom told me the name; he was right, I had never heard of them.

"And she was no virgin. I tell you I was shocked. When I was her age I was in school or playing basketball. I was scared of girls —girls are way ahead of boys, Annunzio. She was wearing this bra made of wire and filled with plastic foam. I said, why do you want to wear a thing like that? You're not *sick*. You're not *mutilated*. She said she had small breasts. She said she used to stuff handkerchiefs under her blouse when she was little. When she was little! She said, My breasts are too small. No one likes girls with small breasts. And I was going out of my skull. All I wanted was to bite in and suck. All I wanted was one little, sweet little breast to suck on. They looked like a couple of peeled pears." he added.

Dom had stopped by a litter barrel. He drank the last of the beer and stuffed the bottle in among the trash, then he put on his jacket and we continued down the empty street toward my apartment.

"She fucks with one of her classmates from the private school. Everyone does it, it's all the rage over there. I asked her how she got started. She said her boy friend why-notted her. I asked her what that meant. She said, he kept asking me why not, why not, why not? She couldn't think up an answer to that one, so they began screwing. Like I said, she's not too bright. The mother is one of these elegant bitches with three husbands. The first one got out just after Pam was born. Pam calls him her *putative* father— isn't that a nice word? Her supposed father. The third one is the one who runs air lines. The second one writes letters to Pam, sends her money. The kid likes him, calls him her real father."

Dom had halted. He stood quiet, looking at me with vague eyes. "I think I don't feel good," he said waveringly.

"You don't look so good either."

"I think I'm going to puke."

I gave him room. "Why don't you go in the gutter?"

Dom stood on the curb and looked into the gutter for about a minute, but nothing happened. "I guess I'm going to keep it down," he said.

After that I walked very slowly and when we came to my apartment house I had slowed us down until we were not moving at all. Dominick still looked like he was about to throw up. I wasn't going to leave him alone, but I didn't want to take him inside to vomit all over my floor, either.

"The mother said she could have me arrested for corrupting a minor, statutory rape. That's when I laughed in her face and told her off. I told her the kid had been getting it from her playmates all along. What else could I say? She was ready to have me locked up. She's bitchy enough to try it, and rich enough. I offered her a drink. I was drinking, so I offered her a drink. She turned it down so I told her to get out. She just stood there, shivering all over. I told her to get out, told her I hadn't invited her daughter and hadn't invited her. I told her that if she wanted to keep her daughter home, then that was fine by me. Put her on a leash, I said. But why bother me about it? I told her she was too curious about the size prick her daughter was chasing. Anyway, I started to get undressed. She looked frightened but she just stood there, trembling. I unbuckled my pants and she clutched her coat shut and her eyes got big. I said, I want to take a bath to wash away the filth, the stinking filth—"

Dominick hesitated and now he gave a soft moan. He stared at me, his face looking like it was smeared with gray paint, then he wheeled away and bent over. I listened to it splashing in the gutter; he was really pumping it out. After a while everything was quiet and slowly he straightened up. He looked stiff and cold and he smelled of vomit. "I think I'm all right now," he murmured.

17

Dominick went into the bathroom and I put a pot of water on the stove to make some instant coffee, too tired to bother with the real stuff. After a time he returned looking pale and empty; he held onto the table and lowered himself cautiously onto the chair, as if a sudden gesture would rattle his insides. He tasted the coffee, relaxed.

"That's a lovely bathroom you have," he said quietly.

"I'm glad you like it."

He sipped at his cup for a while. "The can is especially lovely. They don't make them that way any more, with the chain and all. That's real workmanship."

"I know. It's an antique."

He looked idly at the postcards on the wall, sipped his coffee. "I ought to take a bath. Do you mind if I take a bath?"

"Maybe you ought to stay here overnight."

"I was getting around to that. But I didn't want to put you out, you know."

"You can sleep on the cot. I want to go to bed soon," I told him. "I have to get up and go to work tomorrow."

"Don't let me keep you. I'll go take my bath."

While Dom was in the bathroom I took a blanket and a fresh sheet from the closet and dropped them on the cot. I didn't own a second pillow. I washed the cups and set them in the drain rack, stood the empty milk bottles in the hall outside my door, then took the garbage and trash down to the basement. I was getting hungry, so I made myself a sandwich and ate it over the sink. At last I undressed, got into my pajamas and bathrobe, and sat in the living room to wait for Dom. He was running the water again and it sounded like he was about to take a second bath. I wished I had something to read. Usually I borrowed books from the library or got them from friends, but I didn't have anything on hand. There was Webster's dictionary (1939); a copy of the current *Farmer's Almanac;* the New Testament (Revised Standard); an Italian missal; a beautiful old *Divina Commedia* which fit into the palm of my hand; paper-bound copies of Cellini's *Autobiography* and Thoreau's *Walden;* the two-volume edition of *Cape Cod* (1904) bound in green cloth and stamped with gold, the margins decorated with wistful water-color prints which reminded me of the pictures I used to find in summer cottages when I was a boy; and a big flat volume of Muybridge's photographs of the human figure in motion. I listened to the water draining out of the tub, then the bathroom door opened and Dom came out. He had a towel around his waist and he was carrying a twisted clump of wet laundry. I would have figured Dom to be hairy, but he wasn't; his chest was as bald as a sausage. "I thought I might as well wash out some of my clothes," he said. "Where can I dry them?" We laid his socks on the radiator, then hung his shirt over the back of a chair, draped his undershirt and shorts from the rungs and shoved it alongside the radiator, too. He looked tired but he didn't seem sick any more. He unfolded and refolded the sheet and slowly began to make the cot.

"Annunzio, do you know how God created the world?"

"No," I said.

"He shit it."

I said it was news to me.

"God shit the world. That's why it stinks. That's why we're so miserable here, crawling around on this giant dunghill, this huge globular turd." He began unfolding the blanket.

"How did you find out?"

"It came to me in a vision. God shit the earth and made us out of it." He folded the blanket lengthwise, then laid it on the sheet and began to tuck the edges under the mattress. "Did it ever occur to you that our precious bodies are mere bags of shit? We're born in it, we die in it. We leave a trail of excrement behind us."

"That may be."

He turned to face me. "But you don't believe it about yourself." His voice was resentful, accusing. "And you don't want to believe it about anyone else, either. You forget so easily that we all stink. We *reek*. I never forget it," he added.

"Good for you."

"I'm clean. Look." He spread his arms wide, then let them drop. "I'm cleaner now at this moment than anyone I know. I've vomited and pissed and shit. I've taken a bath. All you others are still crammed full, stinking and slimy." He sat on the edge of the cot, peered at me. "You know what's wrong with you?"

"No. What's wrong with me?"

"There's not enough crap in your life." He looked firm and almost smug. "It's too clean."

"A lot you know about my life."

"And that is why you will not see the face of God. Not until you take one of your women and have her sit astride your chest, facing your feet. Then, if she bends forward, way down—"

"Where do you get these visions?"

"I know my catechism," he said. "I know who made me."

"He made you with a marvelous filthy mind."

"You know what's wrong with you?"

"You already told me."

"You own too much," he said.

"Me? I own too much?"

"You own this pad, don't you? You own this rug, don't you? Your hands are full, you're loaded down. You're beginning to get scared you'll drop something. You're getting old."

"I'm going to bed." I stood up.

"Do you ever think about death?" he asked abruptly. He looked at me, waiting for my reply.

"Of course I think about death."

"What are you doing about it?" He was still watching me, intent.

"I'm living." I could not think of much more. "I'm keeping alive the best way I know how."

Dom looked very disappointed. "That isn't enough," he said listlessly. He sank back and stretched out on top of the blanket.

"I'm still learning." My answers sounded feeble, even to me. "What I mean is, I don't actually think about death but I brood about it and then go do something else. I don't know what I think. I'm tired."

"Christ, I forgot about these paintings. I'll have nightmares if I sleep in here." He made a grimace and flung his arm over his eyes.

I told him he would have pleasant dreams.

"Don't you ever get tired of painting cunts?" he asked from under his arm.

I said no. I left for the bathroom and when I returned Dominick was sitting cross-legged on the cot, an ash tray in his lap, smoking a cigarette. I asked did he want me to wake him when I got up tomorrow. He said yes. He snubbed the cigarette in the ash tray and set it on the floor. I told him I didn't care how long he stayed up, but I was going to bed now.

"Are you ever afraid of dying?" he asked.

"Yes."

He looked puzzled. "Are you afraid of the pain, or the going out, or what?"

"I don't know. Everything, I guess."

"I want to live forever." He smiled gently, apologetically. "Sometimes I think I'm going to be the first person not ever to die. The truth is, deep down inside I believe I am going to live forever. I'll grow old, very old, but I'll *not* die."

"Maybe everyone believes that."

"I'll grow to be a hundred years old, two hundred, a thousand. I'll be dignified and serene and wise. People will come from all over to ask me questions, and they'll treat me with respect. I'll be invited to weddings. I'll eat olives and drink a little wine, and after dinner I'll play with my grandchildren's great-grandchildren."

Dom once told me that his full authentic name was Domingo Roberto Saltares y Ryan. His mother was born and educated in Ireland, his father was Spanish and had held a lectureship at the University of Barcelona, as well as having been a minor poet and something of a politician. Dominick was born in Barcelona and has childhood memories of the parades there at the start of the Civil War. During the war Saltares and his family crossed into France and made their way to Ireland where they were taken in by the Ryans, but after a year in Dublin, Saltares—who had been teaching at a parochial school—said that he would return to Barcelona rather than look at the face of one more Irish Catholic priest; so they sailed to the United States and Saltares gave lessons in Spanish grammar at a Boston night school for three years before he finally accepted the job which had been offered to him when he first arrived: teaching linguistics at Boston College, an institute founded by the Society of Jesus. Dominick went to the Brookline public schools and later enrolled at Harvard, then during his sophomore year he lost interest and joined the army. In Korea he tried to catch pneumonia by crawling from his tent at night to lie in his underwear in the snow, but eventually he was sent into combat. He told me that the first time he came under fire he thought somebody had made a mistake; he said it was not until five or six rounds had been shot at him that he realized that they were trying to kill him and he began to fire back. After the army he returned to Harvard and although he still had no interest he graduated. I met him some time later. Fitzpatrick said that Dom's metaphysical theories were astigmatic, and Nikos thought that Dom lied too much; they were right, but at least when you listened to Dominick you could tell the true from the false and you could not do that with everybody. Dom was a loner and it was always difficult for me to remember that his parents were living somewhere near Chestnut Hill, or that he had two younger sisters. Dom was my friend and I felt like a priggish ass not telling him about Nancy, but I knew for sure that I did not want to say to him or to anyone else even one word about her.

When the alarm clock woke me I went to the living room and asked Dominick did he want to get up. He mumbled something so I set the alarm for one hour later and slid back into bed. The next time the clock woke me I pushed myself into the bathroom and shaved and when I came out Dom was dressed, seated on the edge of the cot tying his shoes. I telephoned R and R and told Marian that I was going to be a little late this morning. She said she had already figured on that; she told me Scott was not there yet and asked was I sick. I said no, I would be over as soon as I finished breakfast. Dom washed up, then stripped the cot while I fried some bacon and scrambled all the eggs I had. We ate a leisurely breakfast. At that season the sun never reached into the apartment so we had to eat with the kitchen light on; Dominick said he felt heroic, getting up before sunrise. His voice was slow and warm with sleep, and his face somewhat wrinkled. He asked had I believed what he had told me last night. "Some of it," I said. He brooded on that for a while, but I couldn't tell what he was thinking. We talked about my work at Research/Research—the death industry, he called it—and about his job. He was no longer a sub-stitute school teacher. "I don't have a phone in my new place. They can't call me when they need me, so they dropped me from the rolls. Money is getting scarcer every day." He took a slow drink of coffee and then gently sat back and lit his first cigarette, looking at me a long while. "How have you been, Annunzio? You've got a secret—some woman?"

I shrugged and asked him if he was still paying rent at his Cam-bridge apartment.

"That's Gretta's place now. When I quit I let her keep my furni-ture and books—alimony—but I'm not paying the rent. All I took was my sleeping bag and typewriter."

"I always rather liked Gretta," I said.

"I know you rather did. Everyone rather likes her. But I'm the one she wants to live with. Did you ever live with a girl?"

"Never for very long."

"Exactly," he said. "Gretta has a powerful nesting instinct. I was never sure whether she loved me or only my squalid apart-ment. Some women are fascinated by dirt."

"Well, she looks good."

"Oh, yes. I know. All that white blond hair, that elegant neck. She's beautiful like a swan is beautiful. Try going to bed with her some time. It's like mating with a white heron. I'm thinking of founding a monastery with Fitzpatrick," he added.

After breakfast we walked up to Brattle Square together. It was getting on toward eleven but the sun was low and weak and the air was cold. I asked him for his new address; I had a pen and pencil but neither of us had a piece of paper; he told me the address and I repeated it a couple of times.

"You can't miss it," he said. "All the other buildings on the street are boarded up. The bells don't work, so just walk in and go up all the way. Don't mail me anything," he added. "Somebody raids the mailboxes."

"How long do you think you'll be living there?"

He shrugged. "I don't know."

Dom closed his ski jacket around his throat and stuck his hands deep in his pants pockets. He hunched his shoulders and smiled, stamping his feet.

"Take care," I said. I reached out and touched his shoulder, stupidly. I was going to miss seeing him, I knew that. "Take care, Dom."

"You too."

Dominick waved and headed across the street, and I went down Brattle Street to the office.

18

In December the Governor and his assistants left Boston and went up along the Charles River to study the hills, the slack water and gray marshland, to search out the best site for a new town. They chose a place on the north bank and settled there the following spring. They drew a little crisscross of streets close above the water; then moving inland they set aside a stretch for common grazing, put up a long palisade fence, and divided the ground into neat lots. The land was raw, unmade and without shape. The sea mingled with the rocks, grass grew in the river. The soil in the fields was thin, packed with stones, and one valley was lined with clay; the hills were filled with boulders and covered with a tangle of scrub pine, maple, elm, clumps of white birch. At high tide the waters of Cape Cod Bay rose into Boston harbor, flowed upriver, and spread across the mud flats into the marshes, brimming the lowland pastures of the town. They called it Newtown and it was supposed to grow to be the center of government, but the Governor had already taken down his house and moved back to Boston. Those who stayed there set about to possess the land, to reform it, to make it into something. The sachem of the place was dead—his body lay inside a rotting hut frame, encircled by palisade and ditch—so they gave the squaw-sachem £ 10, promised her a coat each winter, and said that they now owned the tract along the river. The money and the coats added up to little in exchange for so much, but the actual cash values did not matter to them. The important thing was the process of striking the bargain, making the exchange, signing the contract. This done, they had a deed of conveyance or release of title, a document of some sort bearing marks and signatures to witness that they and no others held the land because they had made a contract and fulfilled its terms. Thus they knew and their inheritors would know that as God had covenanted with Christ, as Christ had covenanted with them, so they had covenanted with the Indians: the chain was intact and indissoluble. They renamed the town, called it Cambridge, to let the world know where they had been to school. They had put up a meeting house, cleared the fields of rocks, plowed and planted and harvested, ranged their homes two paces from the street and roofed them with board or slate, and now they were building a college. In their eyes the schoolhouse was second only to the meeting-house; once they had reared a place in which to worship God the next thing they looked after was to advance learning and perpetuate it, dreading to leave an illiterate ministry to the church when their present ministers should lie in the dust. They desired above all else to know God, to know His mind. In olden times God had revealed Himself directly, but those disclosures had ceased upon the last phrase in the Bible; now they must read His words, pursue Him through His reflection in that Book. At the utmost they could hope only to glimpse His shadow, to see Him as in a glass, darkly (I Cor. 13:12), for though the words of God were clear, the light of man's reason was weak and clouded with natural corruption. The college was built that the student might strengthen his reason by acquiring rules of logic, and kindle his intellect with natural and moral philosophy, remembering always that the end of his labors was to know God and Jesus Christ, which is eternal life (John 17:3). The scholar might go then from classroom to pulpit and there teach others how to read the words of God with right reason. For sooner or later each man alone turned to the Bible and in secret read. He read it not simply for the sheer facts of history, nor the exhortations and parables, read it not only for delight in the arcane symmetry of Old Testament to New Testament, not only to uncover those prefigurations of the past and future annals of the colony which were hidden in its pages as in a coded almanac, but read it also in an attempt to find some inkling or clue to his own private destiny. He studied its pages like a fretful suitor with a letter from his beloved, watching for salvation or rejection in the turn of a phrase. For in one timeless instant his God not only conceived both the creation and destruction of the universe, but also foresaw the inevitable run of each as yet uncreated life and in that same instant predestined each one to an eternal afterlife in His heaven or hell, predestined each one personally, not as reward or punishment to the life He foresaw for each, but predestined simply by His unknowable and unchangeable sovereign whim. God would have doomed them all to hell, but the Son had struck a bargain with the Father: Christ to descend to earth and become flesh and be crucified in exchange for some chosen by God to rise to heaven. God would have doomed them all to hell because He foresaw the Serpent tempt Eve to the forbidden tree, foresaw her take the fruit thereof and eat, foresaw Eve give it to Adam, foresaw him eat, and in Adam and Eve the entire race lay nestled, sinful and damned. God could have doomed them all to hell, but instead He entered into the covenant with Christ and fulfilled His part of the bargain by choosing this soul, or maybe that one, to be saved from eternal fire. Each man turned then to peer into his soul, hoping to discover some mark of salvation. There was no sure way of telling whether you had been left to hell or elected to heaven, yet the soul unfolded day by day and if you were clear-sighted you might discern God's imprint on your life. God was remote, but the hand of God was everywhere. He guided the season and the plowshare; He had sown the countryside with stones and He could, if He would, make it yield bread. In the end there was nothing to do but work. A man could not work his own salvation, but he could shape the land to the terms of the covenant and shape his life to reveal signs of grace. He took to the land. He feared God, saw in the supple gestures of his wife the serpent which had invaded her flesh to tempt him still, but he turned to the land with love. He trod carefully, knowing that the earth stretched tight and thin as a maidenhead over the mouth of hell. He came to know it, the chaste rigidity of that soil. He took it to himself with caution, then harshly, and at last with madness and despair. He flung himself upon it, emptied himself, then took it again and again until he saw before him— supine and tranquil and unyielding—all he had come to regard as his own. Season after season he went to the fields, fulfilling the covenant unto the last jealous embrace. Now the earth was his and a wilderness no more. For the land was brought into bounds and a time appointed to each thing: the sea rose in its tides and did not trespass. The springs were clear and the stones which cobbled the fields had been drawn away and made to wall in the pastures. Wolf and catamount were banished; oxen, swine, and sheep knew their places. Every March the white ice melted on the river bank and salmon returned to the falls; perch and pickerel swam in Mystic Lake, alewives ran in the Menotomies, grass grew thick on the common, and apple trees flowered in their brief season; sea gulls cleansed the river, the weir was built, oyster shoals were marked and seeded, rows of Indian corn stood in the fields, barley was gathered and heavy squash; gray ducks did not forget the way to Waterfield, and in the hot, windless afternoon imperial pheasants with speckled wings sank down to rest at the edge of the long brown meadows.

19

Nancy came in with snow on her coat.

"It's finished," she said. She started to smile, but her face remained stiff and white.

"What happened? What's wrong?" I was scared to touch her. "What's wrong?"

"Nothing. It's all over. Nothing's wrong." She faced me again.

"What happened?" I touched her cheek. "Why don't you sit down? Take off your coat."

"Can I borrow a handkerchief?"

I ran into the bedroom and came back with a fresh handkerchief. Nancy sat down, dried her eyes, and blew her nose. She said her friend in Manhattan had just telephoned her. "It was awful," she said. "But it's finished."

I began to laugh but then she looked bewildered.

"Do I look a mess?" she asked, thinking I had laughed at her.

"You look beautiful," I said. "Now take off your coat. This friend of yours, whatever his name is—"

"I told you his name," she said. Then she told it to me again.

"This former friend of yours, did he upset you?"

"He said he had just received my letter, the one I said good-by

in. He said I owed him an explanation. He said I could *not* just
stop seeing him, stop writing to him." She hesitated.

"What else did he have to say?"

"He wanted to know who I had fallen for. Those were his
words. He made it so *cheap*. He said there must be somebody else
and he wanted to know who. He kept begging me not to hang up.
He said he had a right to know."

He had never sounded very lovable to me.

"I said I wasn't going to tell him one thing or another. I told
him it was my life and I wanted him out of it. He said he had a
right to know your name. Tell me his name, at least his name. I
didn't tell him. The thought of him knowing about us—" She
winced and shook her head. "I didn't tell him anything. I didn't tell
him anything at all." She looked at me and smiled, but her face
was still pale.

"I foresee a long and happy life ahead of him," I said.

Nancy was peering into her purse and now she pulled out a big
square of paper and handed it to me: the head and shoulders of a
young man—*Best Regards, Tom* or *Dick* or *Stan* or some name
like that. He had small eyes with pale irises, his skin was bland, his
hair cut close to the skull; the thick tweed shoulders looked powerful and the smile was self-contained, modest. It was a face I could
have learned to hate. I turned it sideways and tore it in half, slid
the two halves together and tore them in half, then went into the
kitchen and dropped the pieces onto the garbage in the pail under
the sink. From her purse Nancy had dumped a stack of old en-
velopes onto her lap and was squaring them between her hands
like a deck of cards. She looked up, gave me the pack of letters.

"That's all there is," she said. "He wasn't much of a corre-
spondent."

I took the letters into the kitchen and stuffed them into the garbage, wedging them into the pieces of photo and broken egg shell,
grapefruit rind, coffee grounds. I closed the garbage bag and rolled
the top down as tight as I could, then shoved the pail and all back

under the sink. I washed my hands and returned to the living room.

"Also this," Nancy said. She handed me a key. "It was in with the letters."

She closed her purse and slid it on the trunk beside her books, then drew her legs onto the cot and leaned back against the wall. She looked tired, drained.

"The beach house on Cape Cod?" I asked her.

"No. His apartment in New York."

I flipped it over a few times in my hand—a long brass key with a sawtooth edge—then tossed it into the trash barrel. "Anything else?"

"No," she said. "That's all there is. Or was."

She smiled a little and pushed back a strand of hair. She was wearing her black sweater, the one with the V-neck, and I could see the soft notch of her collarbone and the smooth flesh. She leaned forward and removed her shoes, placed them side by side on the floor, then folded her legs up on the cot again and leaned back against the wall, relaxed. She looked up and saw me watching her and smiled hesitantly. "Is something wrong?"

"No. Not at all." My voice sounded odd to me. I walked down the room, wondered what I was doing, and walked back. There was a distant rattling sound which was coming closer and closer, then the radiator rumbled and came snap snap CLANG SNAP HISSS —a thick jet of water shot toward the ceiling and wavered, falling in spray against the drapes. I had run over to turn the valve but by now the radiator was dancing wildly, a blur of cast-iron grape leaves and thumping claw feet. I twisted the valve as hard as I could and for a moment the air was filled with a roaring spray; then it was gone and a sharp metallic stink filled the room. The puddle beneath the radiator began trickling across to where the floor boards were rotted through. I felt embarrassed. "It's an old radiator," I said apologetically.

"How often does it do that?"

"Whenever the heat comes on."

Nancy smiled, pushed up her sleeves; the color had come back to her face and she looked happy. I walked over and sat beside her and looked at her legs, at the dim gold shadow where the stocking was more thickly woven along the heel and across the toe.

"You're wearing stockings," I said. That was a nothing remark but I couldn't think of what to say. "They're so thin I hadn't noticed."

"They're not very warm, but they're warmer than bare skin."

I put my hand on her ankle. It was cool and when I closed my hand I felt the invisible screen of the stocking and then her flesh, the tendons and bone.

"Do you have to work tonight?" I asked. "Something you have to study?"

"No. Not really. I did most of it this afternoon."

We sat there quietly. My mouth had gone dry. Then I reached across her and picked up the two red books she had left on the trunk: the little one was an Anglo-Saxon text and the big flat one was a collection of Anglo-Saxon translations. I opened the little one and looked at the poems. I couldn't decipher a line but I liked the shape to some of the letters. Everything was stilled, quieted.

"Speak to me in Anglo-Saxon," I said.

"I can't speak it. I can only read it. And I can't do that very well either."

"Can you read this?"

She leaned close to see where I pointed at a line, her hair burning against my cheek.

"Well, if you let me peek at the vocabulary at the end of the book I could probably decode it." She turned her head and looked at me, an inch away.

"Talk to me in Anglo-Saxon."

She leaned back and smiled. "They don't teach us to talk it. It's a one-way language. You always translate out of it, into something else."

"Tell me a word."

She hesitated. "What word?"

"Any word at all."

While she paused to think I looked at her eyes, the fragile eyelids and lashes, trying to memorize them.

"Hond," she said, turning her hand palm-upward. "That means hand."

"That's easy. I could have guessed that one."

She thought a moment. *"Heorte.* That means heart."

I told her to say some more.

"Ferth. That means heart, too. Or mind. Or spirit." Her voice was soft, tentative.

I didn't say anything.

"Ferth-loca. That's the enclosure of the heart, where the heart is." She touched her fingers to her breastbone. "Or where the spirit is."

I took that hand and slowly kissed her palm and looked up to find her watching, wide-eyed.

"It's a good language," I said.

"What? Oh! Yes."

Suddenly I had this great urge to run around. "What's it like outside?" I asked her.

"Outside? Snowing. It was about four inches deep. It was lovely," she added.

"Would you like to go out for a walk?"

"All right. If you want to. Yes."

So we did.

20

Michelle had her baby. I telephoned the hospital and asked if she could have visitors; they said yes and told me the hours and I went over the next afternoon. The maternity ward was cheerful-looking. The walls were bright, doors were open, people standing around the beds were talking and laughing, and along the hallway there were paper bluebirds and one big paper stork had its bill clamped on a diaper with a baby tucked inside peeping out at you. I saw a nurse seated at a little desk, so I showed her my pass and asked her how to find Mrs Bretton. It sounded fake to hear myself saying Mrs Bretton. The nurse smiled, put aside her pen, and led me down the hall. She gave me a friendly glance.

"Are you the father?"

"No."

She rapped gently on a door, then opened it and slipped inside. I hear her say, "You have a visitor, Mrs Bretton." A moment later she opened the door and let me in. Michelle was propped up in bed; a bottle of clear fluid hung by the wall and a long tube ran from it down into the lower part of her arm. She looked awful.

"Ah, Frank." She made a smile. "How good of you to stop by."

"You look well," I said. "How are you feeling?"

The nurse glanced at me. She lifted Michelle's shoulders and plumped up the pillows, moved to the window and adjusted the blinds to let in more light, then looked at me once more and left.

"The nurse is wondering who you are," she said.

"She mistook me for Ralph."

I smiled, but Michelle gave me a haggard look and said nothing.

"So," I said. "How are you?" Her face was gray.

"I'm all right now, I guess. I was hemorrhaging again last night."

"Oh. Well, you look fine now." I tried to sound hearty.

She smiled crookedly. "Yes. I can imagine. Especially in this outfit." She plucked at the sloppy hospital gown with her free hand.

Michelle was a thin, flat girl. She had a handsomely angular face and she knew how to dress and how to arrange her hair, but when she was disarrayed she looked a mess.

"Well. How's the baby?"

"The baby? The baby is all right." She gestured at a photo which stood on the table beside the bed. "That's the baby."

I picked up the photo; it showed the profile face of a baby, the head covered with shaggy black hair. "Is it a boy or a girl?" I asked.

"A boy. Nothing worked out right."

I stood there and studied the picture, wondering what to say. "He looks very healthy," I ventured.

"It's going to be hell," she said curtly. "It's going to be hell trying to bring up a boy."

With her free hand she took the picture and leaned it against the bowl of flowers on the table. Then she reached for a pack of cigarettes, shook one out, picked it up, and placed it between her lips. I found the matches and lit her cigarette.

"Thanks," she said. She lay back with her cigarette and looked

out the window, silent for a while. "A girl would have been simpler," she said later. She shrugged. "I named him Michael."

"That's a nice name."

"Here." She laid the cigarette in an ash tray and handed me a little white card. "Can you read this? I can't. It came with the flowers from Ralph."

It was a line of Latin. "It says, some day we'll look back on all this and enjoy it. Something like that."

She frowned, then took the card and tucked it into the corner of the picture frame. "Ralph is in New York."

Ralph did a lot of business in New York; there didn't seem to be anything to say to that.

"How did you find out I was in here?" she asked.

"You said the baby was due about now, so I called your place and the maid told me you were here."

"No one else seems to have found out. You're the only person who's come in. And it seems like I've been here for ages," she added. "Where *is* everybody?"

"Maybe you ought to call them. Or get the maid to do it." I didn't know who her friends were any more, but I knew that I didn't want to get in touch with them.

"Everyone thought I married Ralph for his money. Now they can count the months and have something new to gossip about. All my friends," she said bitterly.

"Forget about them." I shrugged, but she was right about the gossip. I looked around the room, hunting for a way to change the subject. It must have cost a lot: she had a bedside telephone, a television screen set high in the wall at the foot of the bed, elegant furniture, draperies. I moved over to the window and gazed out.

"The best room in the house," Michelle said.

"You sure have a grand view from up here."

"Yes, it is rather."

I stayed at the window, looking out; it was easier than facing her.

"My aunt is coming up. She still doesn't know the real story. She'll be full of hearts and flowers."

I turned to her. "Is there anything I can get for you? Do for you?"

"No. I'll be going home in a few days, anyway. I forgot to ask, how have you been?"

"Oh, I'm all right. Everything is going along well."

She crushed her cigarette into the ash tray, then leaned back and closed her eyes. "I *am* tired." She opened her eyes. "Listen, I'll give you a call sometime."

"I wish you would." I moved around and put on one of my gloves and stood awkwardly at the door. "Well, take care."

Michelle smiled briefly. "Bye-bye, Frank."

So I was back at my apartment earlier than I had planned. Nancy was coming over in an hour. The sky was gray and on the ground the snow was so dirty it looked like ash. I pulled the shades down and closed the drapes, turned on the lights. That was a good way to raise the electric bill, but at least it was less gloomy. Nancy and I were supposed to go visiting on Sunday (first my parents, then on to Concord to her parents) and I was brooding about the complicated transportation arrangements we had made—then abruptly I got the idea of borrowing Beth's automobile. If we had a car everything would be easier. I went out and trotted around to Beth's apartment, a basement flat, and knocked on the glass. Bob opened the door and for a moment we didn't recognize each other. "Oh," he said. "Frank. Come in." All the lights were on. A couple of books lay open on the table along with a big leather notebook, loose sheets of paper, slide rule, coffee cup, and ash tray. "It's Frank," he called out.

"It looks like you've been working," I said.

He shrugged and tossed a big mechanical pencil onto the notebook. "Have a chair. Let me get you some coffee."

I sat at the table. Bob was in his late thirties. He was taller than I was; his hair was short, like a stiff brush, and he had a rather hard-looking face. I think his last name was Carter. He brought me a cup of coffee and sat down.

"What's new?" he asked.

"I came down to ask a favor."

"Anything at all, so long as it isn't money." He didn't smile much.

"I'd like to borrow Beth's car tomorrow."

"Beth," he called out. "Frank wants to borrow your car." He turned back to me. "She's taking a bath."

I had figured she was taking a bath. She was always taking a bath. She was the cleanest person I had ever known.

Beth said she would be right out.

"What's going on?" I gestured at the sheet of paper on which there were columns of numbers, each one headed with a Greek letter.

"Just the usual stuff I didn't have a chance to finish at the office," he said.

We drank our coffee and listened to the water draining from the bathtub. Bob picked up the mechanical pencil and worked it aimlessly a few times. It had colored buttons around the top and when you pressed one down the shaft you got a colored lead at the point: black, red, green, blue. Suddenly he rapped the pencil against one of the books and looked at me with a slight frown. "Ever read this?" he asked.

The title said something about psychology; it looked dull. I admitted that I had not read it. "But it looks interesting," I added.

"Human engineering," he said sharply. "It works too."

"I suppose you use a lot of that on your job."

"It *is* my job."

I turned the pages of the book and said I would have to get it from the library and read it.

The bathroom door opened and Beth came out. She was wearing her white robe, the one that was made of terry cloth, and her hair was wrapped in a white towel. "Hi there," she said, smiling. Beth was happy because she had just taken a bath and because Bob and I were in the room together, waiting for her.

"Frank wants to know if he can borrow your car," Bob said.

"Sure." She took a set of keys from the big ceramic bowl on the cabinet. "Going to visit your folks?"

"Yes."

"Catch." She tossed me the keys.

I said thanks. Beth turned to the stove and tapped the side of the coffee pot with her fingers, testing for heat. "And after that I'll be driving out to Concord," I said.

"Taking somebody with you?" Bob asked.

"A girl," I said.

He seemed amused. He began to straighten up the papers, smiling a little to himself. Beth poured herself a cup of coffee and sat down with us at the table.

"Beth is moving," Bob said. "Did she tell you?"

"No," I said. "I haven't really talked with her in a long time."

"Yes," he went on. "She's moving out at the end of the month."

Beth turned up the collar of her robe, tucked it closer across her breasts and smoothed away some wrinkles. Her face was polished, and as blank as if she were deaf.

"Where is she moving to?" I asked him.

"One of the apartments in the building where I live is vacant. She's moving in there."

"Does she know about this?" I asked.

"She signed the lease," he said.

"I take it you'll be getting married soon," I said to him.

"Hoho," Beth said.

Bob shrugged. "These things take time. But she's improving."

"Do either of you comedians have a cigarette?" Beth asked.

Bob took a cigarette pack from his breast pocket, gave her one, then lit it for her with his lighter. The cloth above his pocket was marked with gray scratches and he had a couple of pencils clipped in there.

"What's new with you, Frank?" she asked.

"Nothing much."

"Nothing much at all?"

"Everything is just about the same," I said.

"How's the painting going?"

"I haven't done any since last summer."

"Well," she said brusquely. "Good luck with the girl."

"Thanks." I stood up. "I've got to get moving."

"See you around," Bob said.

He turned back to his work, smiling to himself, then I left and Beth locked the door behind me.

21

It snowed again today. When I went out this morning the sun was like a clear piece of glass, then it grew tarnished and the sky turned ashen. For a while the near mountains stood white, with nothing in back of them, then the southwest peak began to look as if it were made of fog and a minute later it blurred and mixed with the sky. After that you could see how all the mountains were dissolving, and by the time I reached Common Street they were gone and the sky was empty. I went to the press, read all the headlines, and finally bought a paper. "Going to be a big one," said Claude. I told him I hoped so. At least it would give us something to watch, I said. A while ago I came back from mailing some cards and the air was stilled, with the snow deep and the stars burning in silence. It was pleasant to walk across the campus under the loaded trees. The emptied dormitories were dark, and above each door there was a lighted lamp and a column of lighted windows going up with the interior stairway, but everything else was blacked out. Then our house loomed over the hill like a stranded ark, top-heavy and canted, every window blazing with light.

When I came in my wife and the Parovs were standing in the

front hall, talking with Evan Miller, and a big fir tree was sprawled on the stairway behind them. I asked what was going on.

"Evan bought the tree," my wife said. "But it's too big for his apartment."

"He wants us to take it," Ruth said. She was wearing her black tights and a loose jacket which came down to her thighs; she dresses that way after her kids are in bed. She hasn't a bad figure, actually, and her evening get-up always adds a little exotic charm to the house.

"Why not?" Evan asked.

"I think we ought to get it up here in the hall," Ruth said. She turned to us. "What do you think?"

"Where in the hall?" I asked her. The hall looks like a junk shop—it has the Parovs' baby stroller, two pairs of skis and poles belonging to the Meisterburgs, Evan Miller's mahogany lawn chair, the Bushes' spare snow tire, the Taylors' bicycles, PJ Kelley's trunk, half a cord of firewood which we share with the Parovs, and some things that belong to the house: a baby carriage, three snow shovels and a push broom, a couple of badminton rackets, and a bagful of dead tennis balls.

"Maybe we could auction off some of this stuff," my wife said.

"Who would buy?" Dimitri asked.

"Why don't you take it?" I asked him. "Set it up in your living room."

Dimitri shrugged. "We don't have enough ornaments to decorate a tree this big." His sweater was inside out. It got inverted whenever he pulled it off; tomorrow it would be right-side out.

Evan told the Parovs they could have his ornaments; I told Dimitri he might as well take it.

"All right," he said reluctantly. Evan and I helped him wrestle the tree off the stairs and into the Parovs' apartment, accidentally crushing a few branches against the narrow doorway so that the air blossomed with the frosty odor of pine.

The house is quieting down now. My wife is asleep, and the

baby inside her is curled on himself like a fist. The Meisterburgs arrived a while ago, the motor of their little car ticking madly as a two-dollar watch. The front door swished open, crashed shut, and their boots clattered across the hall and mounted along the stairway, turned booming through the second-floor hall, mounted the next stairway, and grew dim, vanished. A moment later their apartment began to send its faint signals: a stress passing from floor board to beam to joist, a muffled creak descending the wall, a compression in the sills, the vibration of shifting cargo. Robert Meisterburg teaches political science. He grew up in Wisconsin, came East to get his B.A., and went to England to get his Ph.D. He met Penelope Mason when she was over there at the London School of Economics, and he married her; Penny's father is very big in Washington. Robert once asked me if I wanted anything in life; I laughed and said yes, and asked him what he wanted. "Power," he said hotly. Robert knows I'm a painter and he assumes I'm a wastrel. He cannot conceive that I might want my sort of power as much as he wants his, cannot believe that I would like to force my vision on everyone's eyes. Frederick and Sally Bush took showers: a steady murmurous ringing in the water pipes, then silence; again the long murmurous ringing, then silence. They live right over our front half. The sounds from their apartment faded bit by bit, revealing at last the faint tap-tap of Patrick John Kelley's typewriter. PJ is thin and jumpy and spends every night typing on a dissertation about the contemporary English novel; it's over seven hundred pages long and each time he makes a revision it gets longer. One of these nights PJ is going to crack up.

22

What am I to say of Nancy and how am I to speak of her? I could tell you about myself, a story of furnished rooms, from a watertight cabin in Kennebunkport through East Baltimore Street to an oven with a slatted door in Jacksonville. I've rented in the city and out in the country. I know the fancy brickwork, the brownstones, the bay windows, the painted clapboards, the shingles and asbestos siding, the uneven steps, refinished lobby, suffocating mansard and gray basement, the dim front hall with three pale oblongs of mail on the table, the dark stairway, bathroom at the end of the corridor—the washbowl with a crack like a wet black hair, the tub with the rusty drain, the orange hose looped over a hook for a makeshift shower—and the room itself with a stringy carpet, stuffed armchair, lamp, bed, and the bureau with its speckled mirror; I've met the widowed landlady, the crooked janitor, the drunk who pisses on the bathroom floor, the old bastard who coughs all night and spits blood in the john—chased off the rats, mice, and roaches who never paid rent. In the Mount Auburn Street apartment my bedroom was a narrow cell with the right wall made of cardboard and the left one of painted brick, a curtained doorway at this end and a jammed-shut window at the other. I had a straight chair, a bureau, a bed, and in the far corner the hollow stump of a missing radiator; I had shut the valve and crammed the pipe with rags, but whenever the heat came on it puffed up little clouds of steam. I met Nancy and everything came apart—the walls fell out and the floor knelt down and the ceiling dissolved to float away as soft and silent as a milkweed cloud. We were marooned on a stretch of white Cape shore, planted codfish beneath the corn to make it grow, dressed Nancy in quahog pearls, painted her picture on birch bark using an inky squid for a brush, and came morning I shaved with a razor clam and we breakfasted on blackfish eggs and beach plums.

Winter ended on Saturday that year and it looked like a good day to ask her to marry me. She came over in the middle of the morning and made breakfast while I shaved and washed. We lingered over our coffee, then Nancy cleared the table and I stripped the bed, stuffed the last sheet and towel into the laundry bag and tucked it under my arm, and we headed out. The air was bright, cool, windy. At the laundry the door was wide open; inside, it smelled clean with the odor of soap and boiling cloth, and the floor shook under the water tubs. We stayed a while to talk with the fat woman there. She must have weighed three hundred pounds, always wore a white dress with a long white apron, and looked herself like a bundle of steaming wash. When we came out it was getting on to noon.

"Let's walk down to the river," I said. We walked along where the bank was flat, where the water brimmed in the grass. Other people were about—a young woman pushing a baby carriage, a few couples strolling on the path, a boy scaling stones at the water—not many. We mounted the steps of the footbridge and walked to the top of the arch over the river. I stopped and leaned my elbows on the stone balustrade and looked upstream at the chafed water, the empty trees along the bank, the sparkling roofs and the sky. I turned to Nancy.

"Yes?" she asked.

"Even if they tear down the bridge, at least the river will still be there."

"Yes," she said.

"Will you marry me?"

"Yes."

"You knew I was going to ask."

"I hoped you were going to."

Saint Paul's campanile had begun to sound, the long falling notes mingling now with the blurred sweet chimes of bell towers farther away. I drew Nancy against me by the stones, turned the collar of her raincoat up.

"I have no prospects," I said.

"I think your prospects are good. I think they're great."

A sea gull skimmed past and rose upstream to the wind, riding the stiff breeze to a standstill, went soaring upward. I said a few more words to Nancy, whispered in her ear, then kissed her while her hair blew this way and that about our heads.

23

Miss Cushing was blind. Her hair was white and her joints were frozen stiff, but her eyes had such bright blue centers that it was hard to believe she was blind. On my way downstairs I would stop at her room to say good morning—she was propped in bed, facing the doorway—and she would give me a few words about the weather. "It's cold," she might say. "Sunny but cold. You had better wear a scarf to keep the cold off your lungs. And don't be fooled by the sun. Spring colds are the worst." I said I agreed completely. "And has anyone cleared the ice off the front steps?" she asked. I told her I could take care of that on my way out, then said good-by and rattled downstairs and out the door.

Miss Cushing's place had been built as the last of a long row of joined houses at the bottom of the street by the river. I don't know how she came into it, for though she was talkative and told many stories about herself I was never able to fit them into the same picture. One time she said that her father had owned a wharf on the river in those days when ships used to sail upstream to Cambridgeport, and he had been a rich man, but another time she said that she had done some sewing for Isabella Stewart Gardner who wore different colored wigs to match her various gowns; she also told me that when she was a young girl William James had bought her a bag of sweets at Billings & Stover, and that she had run the rooming house for generations. One of her special tales was about how she had gone to visit her sister one week and returned on Sunday morning to find the stairway strewn with ladies' undergarments, the second-floor bathtub bobbing with empty champagne bottles, and a young girl asleep on the third-floor landing clad in a black silk ascot necktie and a thin coat of gold leaf. Later someone told me the same story about a different Cambridge rooming house, but maybe Miss Cushing had the authentic version. Most of her life she had lived in the ground-floor apartment and had rented single rooms in the upper stories to students and working gentlemen. Then her eyes dimmed. Faces blurred, the windows turned gray, and the floor went black, but she continued to move about in the shadowy chambers until the morning she rose from bed, tripped, broke her nose, rolled over, and lay on her back staring up into the darkness, not knowing whether it was day or night. After that she grew timid. She abandoned the apartment and moved into the room on the second floor, safe from prowlers and close to the comforting sounds of her lodgers. She received weather reports from the radio on her bedtable and from the chatty nurse who came by each morning. The nurse straightened her up, made breakfast and set out a light lunch, went off; then late in the afternoon a frail quiet woman came in with a few groceries, prepared dinner, cleared the room, and left. Now the house stood alone. The sagging tenements across the street had been evacuated, and the other houses in Miss Cushing's row had already been torn down—the cellars crammed with rubble, pressed flat, and smoothed over with blacktop for use as a parking lot—so that as you walked to the river you saw only the silhouette of that single building, the slate mansard roof and the smooth gray blank where the house next to it had joined. The front hall led past her disused apartment, and at the second and third floors, beneath the wall

switch, there was an ivoried card with faded script: THE LAST MAN
IN WILL PLEASE TURN OFF THE LIGHTS.

I had a narrow room on the third floor and Arieh Gershom lived
across the hall. Arieh had come from Israel to study in Cambridge,
and through some misinterpretation of life here he had brought
with him a number of white flannel trousers which he wore all that
winter and spring. He was taking a string of philosophy courses; he
was bright, could be charming, but he had a gloomy temper and
seemed lonely and at times very unhappy. Now and again when I
headed out to work in the morning he would still be at his desk,
the shades still down and the lamp on, writing a poem. Saturday
nights he usually had a girl in his room, the voice differed from
week to week, and a couple of times the perfume odor was so clear
on the landing that Miss Cushing must have caught it even through
her sleep. One night Michelle—gentle, angular Michelle—and I
happened to step into the hall just as Arieh and a girl appeared at
the top of the stairway. "Stay and have a drink," he said. We were
on our way out, but he looked glum and seemed to want our company. Arieh and I had our whisky in coffee cups so the girls could
drink from glasses; it was pretty awkward, all the way around. He
had been trying to loosen the girl with alcohol but she did not like
the stuff, and now he was getting drunk and rather surly. The girl,
who had fluffy blond hair and a mouth the size of a penny, worked
in an accounting office and appeared to want an apology about
something. When Arieh told her that I was teaching in an art
school she quizzed me about my job, and ended by saying that she
had always thought artists were homos, queers, fairies. It seemed
that she was not about to change her mind. Michelle said a few
words, but it was clear that her French accent irritated the other
girl, who took it to be an affectation, so Michelle buttoned her coat
and sat on the window sill in silence. I hurriedly finished my drink
and we left.

Arieh and I were the only lodgers until late spring when somebody moved into the room next to mine. Her name was Mrs

O'Neil; she had a faint dry voice and a light footfall, and you never knew she had been on the stairway until you heard the door to her room close. Miss Cushing told me the new person's name and confided that it was the first time she had rented to a woman. "But she's been widowed, you know, and it will be a comfort to have her about. Sad. Sad. She is quite nice, isn't she?" Miss Cushing asked. I agreed and let it go at that. I guessed Mrs O'Neil to be about twenty years old, a slight girl with a pallid face and straight brown hair cut brutally short. Arieh told me that her husband had been killed in a car crash about a year ago. He didn't say how well he had known her before she moved in, but I gathered that he had led her to the house and later I was aware that he was no longer taking women to his room.

One night I was awakened by laughter. The laugh began again as a chuckle, chuckle, chuckle, and went wailing higher, dropped into a gasp, then broke into a sobbing, crazy groan. I turned on the lamp and peered into the dim hall. The other doors were shut. The laugh began again and it was Miss Cushing. I crept down to the second-floor landing and called her name into the dark of her half-open door, but there was only the soft chuckling. I reached in, switched on the light. Miss Cushing was propped up in the center of the bed, her crooked hands lay on the blanket like melted candles, her white hair sprawled all over the pillow, and her eyes were staring. When I called her name again she tilted her head toward me. "John?" I said no, and told her my name. "Uncle John? Are you there, Uncle John? Uncle John." I told her my name and explained that I was one of the roomers from upstairs. She waited, her eyes growing bright with tears. "Will *some*body please tell me what I am doing here?" she pleaded. "Will *some*body please explain? Why am I here? Why am I *lying* here?" Then her head flopped back on the pillow. I asked her if she wanted me to get her a glass of water. She slowly shook her head and said no, she wasn't thirsty. I asked did she want me to call her doctor, but she shook her head very wearily. I waited and asked again, but her eyes had closed and she seemed asleep, and as I watched I listened and heard her ragged breathing, so after a time I switched off the light and went back upstairs. Arieh was wide-eyed, his dark chest visible between the open folds of his robe, his hand still on the doorknob to his room. "What happened? You look white in the face," he said. I told him that I didn't really know. "Come in," he said. So I got my bathrobe and crossed into his room. Mrs O'Neil was huddled deep in the armchair by his desk, wrapped in a blanket which concealed all but her face and the slender hand beneath her chin. "You know Rita," he said to me. I said, "Yes. Hello." She answered hello, but she had no smile and she looked uncomfortable, cold. Arieh asked again what had happened, so I told him.

"She's going crazy," Rita said dryly. "She's afraid they'll take her to a hospital or one of those nursing homes. She wants to die here. That's all she ever talks about."

Arieh suggested that we have a drink. "It's three in the morning," Rita said irritably. I told Arieh that I was too tired to enjoy a drink, said good night, and went back to my room. Everything stayed quiet, and a while later I fell asleep.

That summer we began going to the Casablanca. Rita taught ballroom dancing in the afternoon and evening at the Ace Dance Studio, and once or twice a week Arieh would invite me to come with him to meet her when she finished work. We would walk down to Western Avenue and wait in the foyer, then the three of us would taxi back to the Square for drinks. Someone always joined our table: one of Rita's friends, or Arieh's friends from the graduate school, or a young married couple named Kemp who knew Michelle and thought they knew me, or their friend Mark Coulter, or the young man with whom he shared an apartment. The Kemps' marriage was coming apart and they must have been in the Casablanca almost every evening. Carl Kemp was a lawyer who worked in the trust department of a Boston bank; Sally Kemp wore a lot of make-up and her hair was usually mussed. They both looked tired. One night I was standing at the bar when Sally waved, beckoning me to their table. I took my bottle and glass and went over. "Tell us a joke," she said. "Make us laugh."

"I don't know any jokes," I told them.

"Poor Mark," Sally said. "He's dying, you know."

I laughed. "What's he dying for?"

"He's just dying," she said.

Carl looked at his wife in disgust. "That was stupid," he said. "You didn't have to say that."

"He might as well know. He's liable to say something. Besides, everyone knows it."

"I don't understand," I said.

"It's his blood," Carl said apologetically. "Something is wrong with his blood. They keep giving him transfusions but it doesn't do any good."

"It's cancer," Sally said flatly.

"We don't know that for sure," he told her.

"Well, I do."

I did not know Mark well, and after that I did not try to know him any better. I had heard that he had received his law degree but instead of moving on to his bar exam he had taken a job as research assistant to one of his former professors. He was slender, with mild eyes and copper-olive skin, and his hands appeared fragile, leaflike. Sometimes he looked weary and I recalled that I had once advised him to take a vacation, to lie on the beach in the sun. He had gazed at me a moment, rather thoughtfully, then had made a languid gesture and said he was only working afternoons. Now when he was around I watched what I said, and tried to carry on as before. I wasn't much good at it. One night I was standing at the end of the bar with the Kemps and Mark Coulter.

"It's near closing time," Sally said. "Let's have another."

"You don't need another," Carl said.

Sally had already signaled the barman. "More of the same," she told him.

"You've had plenty," Carl said.

"A little Scotch and water never hurt anybody."

Carl turned back to Mark and me. "What were we talking about?" he asked.

"Nothing important," I said.

Mark was looking intently into his glass; his forehead and jaw were glistening with sweat, as if from the effort of concentration. "Clothing," Mark said at last. "We were talking about clothes."

"You have a hairy chest," Sally said, looking at me. "Did anyone ever tell you that?"

"No," I said. "I don't recall anyone saying that."

"It's beautiful," she said.

"Everybody has hair on his chest," Mark told her slowly.

"Well, I don't have hair on *my* chest," she said. "My husband doesn't have hair on *his* chest. Show them your chest, Carl. Take off your necktie, unbutton."

"She goes for men with hairy chests," Carl explained, ignoring her. "She probably thinks it's a sign of bravery."

"Well, I'm not brave," I said. "Not if I can help it."

"Mark is the only brave one," Sally said.

Mark slowly lifted his glass and drank, then set it down and gazed tranquilly ahead of himself, calm and blind to us. His roommate had come up, and now he put his hand lightly on Mark's back to get his attention. "You want to head back to the apartment?" the roommate suggested.

"Might as well," Mark said, turning.

"We have a car outside," Carl said. "Want a ride?"

"It's a nice night," Mark said. "Might as well walk."

After they had left, Carl and I stood at the bar while Sally finished her drink.

"Can't anyone do something?" I asked him.

"No." He compressed his lips, frowning, irritated.

"But what about us?" I insisted. "What are we supposed to do?"

"He says he wants to keep going. He told me he just wants to work and have a few drinks in the evening with his friends." He shrugged his shoulders.

"Mark keeps our spirits up," Sally said humorlessly.

"Doesn't anyone around here feel anything?" I said.

"Yes," she said, turning her disheveled face toward me. "Yes," she said bitterly. "We feel. Now what? We've known Mark a lot longer than you have. Now *you* tell us. Now what do we do?"

"All right," Carl told her. "Calm down, calm down. It's time to go back to our love nest."

I lingered at the end of the bar and watched the Kemps leave. A few moments later the lights were turned up, revealing the empty, disordered furniture and a few astonished faces here and there at the tables, then these turned away with furtive gestures, turned to the door and disappeared, and I went home to my room.

24

I was lying face down on my bed, barefoot and stripped to the waist, when there was a gentle knock-knock on my door. It turned out to be Helen Shawn. "Did I disturb you?" she asked, lingering in the doorway.

"Not at all. I was lying here waiting to get hungry, then I was going out to eat. Come in."

Helen stepped in and tentatively closed the door. "Aren't you going to put on a shirt?"

I took my shirt from the back of the chair and turned the chair over to her. She seated herself limply, crossed her hands in her lap, then averted her eyes and glanced around the room while I dressed.

"It's so small," she said faintly. "The room is so small, so narrow."

"I've been thinking of moving out, actually."

"I should hope so." She watched me pull on my socks, tie my shoes. "The whole place gives me the creeps," she added.

"How would you like to go out to dinner?"

She looked perplexed. "I can't. I just stopped by to invite you to a party."

"Thanks. What party?"

"A farewell party. We have to move out in twelve days, because they're going to tear down the house. So we're giving one last party."

"They've been tearing down that house for years, but they never seem to get started."

"This time it's real. The party is Saturday night, eight o'clock. You can bring someone," she added. "There's no limit."

"Who would I bring?"

"How about that little French girl?" She was referring to Michelle.

"We don't see each other any more."

"Poor Frank." She smiled, her eyes tender and mocking.

"Are you doing anything later tonight?"

"I have a date," she said.

"Lucky Helen. Well, how have you been?"

"Very much the same as always." She stood up wearily, then paused to gaze out the window at the river. "Nothing changes. You ought to know that by now."

"You never can tell. Tonight may be the night when everything changes."

"I hope not." She turned from the window. "I'm going out with someone named Bill Bowser, so that he can sell me his car cheap."

"Oh. Anyway, good luck."

She took a last glance around the room, then looked at me. "You really must get out of here," she said.

"I guess I will." I got up and opened the door.

"Now don't forget to come," she said briskly. "This Saturday."

"Eight o'clock."

Helen smiled quickly, then turned and hurried softly down the stairs, her thin dress wavering as she disappeared.

25

The house where Helen and her roommates lived was in Spring Court, a tiny enclave off Mount Auburn. When the first streets thereabouts were drawn the house stood in the angle between Crooked and Spring, but Crooked Street was straightened out and Spring became Mount Auburn, new houses were built on the realigned lots, then these houses were replaced by larger tenements which were in turn supplanted by the tall brick apartments whose backs now formed the walled boundaries of the court. In summer the sun just reached into the enclosure, but the rooms remained always in shadow. The house itself was about two hundred years old, red clapboard with a shingle roof, and it looked shrunken with age. The upper floor was untenanted and used only as an attic; the front doorway was narrow and the interior was a set of miniature chambers let in with small windows of uneven glass. Walking inside I was always aware of its closely drawn dimensions, aware that it had been designed for other people, yet the proportions had been retained so well that it was as if without diminishing my own size I had walked down a long perspective and entered a house in which everything was rendered small because of its distance. I had first come to Spring Court one summer evening three years ago, following those directions written by Helen on a page torn from her red leather address book. A young woman had come to answer my knock on the screen door, had said that Helen was out. Another girl appeared behind her, then a young man, and behind them a long girl lying on a sofa propped herself up on one elbow to look. I was invited in, and after that I stopped by Spring Court a couple of evenings a week, at first to see Helen and later to visit whoever happened to be there, talking until one or two or three past midnight, then sleeping under an Indian blanket on the sofa and waking late to have breakfast with whichever girl was out of work that day. I left town that autumn and when I returned Helen's three roommates had been replaced by two others, then they also dispersed, married or discovered fresh jobs, or simply moved to another city, and Helen lived with two new roommates now.

I arrived for the party on Saturday evening at eight o'clock. The fireplace mantel was crowded with little bowls of orange cheese, geometrical crackers, peanuts, potato chips, and some sort of pink paste. At the near end of the room there was a lone table, the white cloth decked with rows of glass cups, but all the chairs had been removed and the rug had been rolled up, shoved behind the sofa. "No one ever comes on time except you," Helen told me. She paused at the mirror, turning to look at her image from the corner of her eye while she threaded a tiny gold earring. "Come into the kitchen. You remember Ruth Cantor." Ruth and I exchanged hellos; she was a short, thin-lipped girl who worked at the Family Research Center. "Do you want to help make punch?" she asked me. I said no. The kitchen table was arrayed with bottles of champagne and brandy, and there was a large white basin filled with slices of glistening peach. Clarissa Cullard, the other roommate, came in. "Hello, Frank," she said, thrusting out her hand. Clarissa had a lumpy face and worked in an ad agency; she always shook hands when we met. "That's a rotten way to treat brandy," Clarissa said, moving to the table.

Ruth's fiancé came in with an immense silvered bowl containing a block of ice; then he and Ruth set about preparing the punch. Other guests soon arrived, appearing at the door alone or in twos and threes, each one smiling and hopeful and expectant, their eyes moving quickly to those who were already in the room. The groups standing here and there in the cool, unfurnished chamber—the men looking tanned, dark above their pale suits, and the women with their flushed cheeks and bare arms—all held for a time the promise of poise and graceful motion that you sense before a ball. In a brief while the floor became crowded and the shadowy air thickened, grew hot, people began to perspire. The groups broke, re-formed and merged, pressed close to the punch bowl to refill a glass, ladling the icy champagne and crescent peaches carefully and with effort. A lot of people I had not seen for a couple of years turned up, and among them was David Solomon, now a doctor of medicine. "No specialty," he said. "I'll be satisfied with general practice. Someone told me you were in Europe."

"That was to visit my grandmother," I said. "Mostly I've been kicking around New England."

"So what have you been doing?"

"Treading water," I said.

Viola Shears came in accompanied by a towering, stoop-shouldered young man. Viola was the girl who had been lying on the sofa the first evening I came to Spring Court. Jonah Royal, the Jamaican poet, was around; he was part Negro, called himself *café-au-lait* colored, and seemed to be making it with Clarissa. Harry and Harriette Cloves were there. Someone had told me that the Cloveses had made plans for a divorce, but that they were sticking together to cover some scandal. Helen said that Harry was on probation and that something had come out in the papers about him and a group of teen-age girls. Philip Munk, someone whose name sounded like Slags, Ralph Bretton, and lovely, angular Michelle arrived together. Munk once spent a year in Italy—he had fallen in love with Naples, he said, and knew *all* about Italian men—and he delighted himself by speaking Italian to me. He was working in a publishing house and now he informed me that as a sideline he was starting up a magazine of the arts, and Slags here was his partner or his protégé or his something. I never caught the man's name—it was Slags or Slagsear—who carried a slender bamboo cane. Someone introduced me to Ralph Bretton, but we did not get along. He was not an easy man to talk with. At one point Helen asked him what he did for a living and he replied that he was a designer. "What do you design?" she asked.

"Life," he said brusquely.

"Oh, that's nice," Helen said.

Michelle had cut her hair since I had last seen her and it was very short now. The haircut, along with her slim, flat body, gave her a boyish appearance, made me more aware than ever of her fragility. We talked a bit: her smile and her gestures seemed brittle, and I was not at ease either. Nikos and Patrick Fitzpatrick showed up, so we three withdrew to the far corner away from the door to talk and drink; later Dave Solomon joined us and for a while we had a private party of our own. I saw Carl Kemp at the punch bowl, but I did not see his wife anywhere. A radiant girl in a white dress started to enter, but the room was packed and for a few moments she was held in the doorway. "Who is she?" Nikos asked. I told him I was wondering that myself. I turned back to the conversation, and when I looked over toward the door again Sally Kemp and Mark Coulter, who was dying, and Coulter's roommate were coming in. Then Gail Falconer came by with John Sentry: she threw her arms around me, kissed me hard on the mouth, drew back, and asked why I didn't come around to visit the old One Hundred any more. One hundred was the street number of the co-operative house where I had lived for six months with Gail and John and seventeen others. When I first saw Gail Falconer she was in a jersey and shorts, sitting in the center of the kitchen table at the One Hundred and laughing wildly at something John had told her; at that time Gail had just finished a course of electric shock treatments. John Sentry arrived with her drink and drew her off. "Where did Nikos disappear to?" I asked.

"He went to find out about the girl," Dave said.

"Maybe she's come to join the mystical body of Cambridge," Fitzpatrick suggested.

"Drinking this stuff is the wrong way to keep cool," Dave said.

Fitzpatrick and I banged on the window frame, loosened it, opened the window some. It didn't make much difference, there was no breeze.

"We're going to be asphyxiated," Dave said.

Nikos returned, edging his way along the wall. "She's from California," he announced.

"And she seeks union with the mystical body of Cambridge," Fitzpatrick added.

"What is this mystical body of Cambridge?" Dave asked him.

"You have to live here to know it," Fitzpatrick said.

Helen squeezed in toward us and said something.

"I can't hear you," I said.

"Do any of you want to go out and get some ice and things?"

"Sure," Nikos said. "I could use the fresh air."

"Ice and what things?" Fitzpatrick asked.

"Supplies," Helen said. "Alcoholic things."

It was great to walk down the street with Nikos and Fitzpatrick, just the three of us walking along in the warm night. It was the best. "Let's keep walking and not go back," I said.

"I could walk to the end of the world," Nikos said. "Right off the edge."

"I'm going home," Fitzpatrick said. "I've had it."

Nikos and I tried to dissuade him, but it was no use, and Fitzpatrick went on to his apartment while we ducked into the liquor store for supplies.

I don't know what time it was when we returned. The kitchen was a mess and Ruth Cantor was arguing with Helen, her voice tense and rushing, abrupt. There was a cluster of stained glassware at the edge of the table, along with a couple of wet ice trays and the silvery innards of a coffee pot, knives, a corkscrew, the drain board littered with bottle caps, ruptured cellophane bags, potato chips, torn cracker boxes, curved slices of red wax, wet paper napkins, empty bottles everywhere—perched on the window sill, under the table, on the rim of the stove—and in the sink a clear pool of water in which floated the fragile outlines of a few ice cubes. I pushed a space clear on the drain board and began to set out the fresh gin bottles.

"What did you tell them to buy *that* for?" Ruth cried. "They won't ever go away if we keep serving drinks." Her face was flushed and her eyes glistened with tears.

"Do you want to go out there and say, go home?" Helen asked her. "Is that what you want? Do you want me to do it?"

"What's happening?" I asked.

Ruth took a breath and compressed her lips, then whirled around and banged her fist on the table top, shuddering the glasses.

"Clarissa's handing out balloons," Helen said. "It's not my fault."

"Well, they don't need balloons," Ruth muttered. "They need to sober up." She thrust the basket into the coffee pot, began hurriedly to spoon in the fresh coffee grounds, scattering them wildly over the disordered table.

Nikos had opened our bag of ice cubes and was pouring them gently into the sink. Then he hefted one of the square gin bottles, studied the seal a moment, cut through it carefully with the point of a corkscrew, and set about making a drink. Ruth slammed the loaded coffee pot onto the stove, lit the gas, and plunged into the living room. "Actually, I'm hungry," I said. Helen quietly moved some empty bottles aside and leaned back on the window sill. "All we have left is lobster paste," she said. There was a light crash and tinkle over the noise in the living room, but no pause in the roaring hubbub, the laughter. Helen slowly closed her eyes. "I'll have one of those," I said to Nikos. I took my drink into the living room and moved to the fireplace mantel where I found a bowl of lobster paste. Beside me Carl Kemp was blowing up a balloon; his forehead was red with effort and his eyes glittered, bulging—suddenly it escaped, shot into the crowd, and flopped softly against the ankle of a girl who shrieked and skipped aside, turning to look at the floor. Someone was shouting: "Rub them against the wall. Friction electricity. If you rub them against the wall they stick there. It's friction electricity." Ralph Bretton and Michelle had gone. Gail Falconer and John Sentry had gone. The Cloveses had gone. Viola Shears and her tall friend had gone. A couple I had never seen before was huddled against the far wall. The man struck a match: she took his wrist, lighted her cigarette, then released him and rolled indolently back against the wall and blew a soft plume of smoke. He leaned forward to kiss her. Mark Coulter, his grave copper face luminous with sweat, sat down languidly in the corner of the sofa. Nikos came over and asked me if there was anything to eat. I was carefully scooping up some lobster paste with a potato chip. "This is all I can find," I said.

"Where's the girl?" he asked. He meant the girl in the white dress.

"She's around. She just left for the bathroom. She has a lot of friends here tonight," I added.

Clarissa Cullard came up. "What did you do with Patrick?" she asked.

"He was afraid he might lose his virginity if he came back," Nikos said.

"Ha!" Clarissa said. "I heard they castrated him when he was an altar boy." She went into the kitchen.

"Vulgar bitch," Nikos murmured.

Just as I finished my drink Helen came over leading a dark young man with delicate, almost fragile features. "Frank, have you met Mr Hassan? Mr Hassan is from Pakistan. Pakistan, you know, is quite different from India."

Hassan smiled politely but said nothing.

"Perhaps you could help him," she said. "He seems to be having difficulty blowing up this balloon." Helen walked off.

"I wouldn't bother about that," I told him. "Have you met everybody?" I turned, but Nikos was slyly moving away. "Have you met Dr Solomon?"

I introduced him to Dave Solomon, then went into the kitchen. Clarissa Cullard was at the sink with her hands in the melting ice and Jonah Royal had pressed in close behind her, his glistening dark arms tight about her waist, whispering into her ear while she moaned and chuckled. I dropped some ice cubes into my glass, picked up a couple of bottles, and returned to the living room mantelpiece. Ruth Cantor and her fiancé were sitting on the sofa drinking coffee; she seemed composed now, sedate, except for a light flush on her cheeks. Ruth chatted earnestly with her fiancé a moment, then turned and said something to Mark Coulter, who smiled gently. The girl in the white dress stood in the doorway listening to Mr Hassan. There was a crash—the table with the silvered punch bowl was askew and a corner of the table cloth hung down like torn bunting amid some rolling glassware. Dave Solomon apologized, and Ruth's fiancé took the bowl into the kitchen. Sally Kemp came up: "I haven't seen my husband once tonight. Have you?"

"He's right over there," I said.

"Don't tell me. Aren't you hot? You look hot." Her make-up was blurred and it looked like her face was flying apart.

"I'm dying."

"Take off your necktie. You don't look good in a necktie."

"Why don't you go get yourself a drink," I suggested. Sally

strolled off toward the kitchen. Ruth Cantor and her fiancé had left the house, the glistening punch bowl in his arms. Slags dropped a balloon lightly in the middle of the empty floor, then swatted it with his cane. Jonah Royal and Clarissa Cullard knelt beside an open suitcase from which she was throwing out stuffed toys—a teddy bear, a horse, a penguin— Helen touched my arm: "Make them stop," she pleaded. Shattering glass cascaded on the window sill, broke, fell to the floor, tinkling. I looked around, trying to make out how it had happened. "It doesn't matter!" Clarissa shouted. "The house is coming down anyway."

"I have to sleep here," Helen said plaintively.

Philip Munk and Slags had come up to Helen. "Good night," Munk was saying. "We must leave now. It's been a lovely party, but it's getting late and Slags here needs his rest."

Helen said good night distractedly.

Munk turned to me. *"Buona notte, Francesco.* Don't hunger so much for the flesh. Oh, it shows, it shows." He patted my shoulder. "And it's one of the seven deadly sins, you know." He leaned back and smiled warmly.

"The least deadly," I said. I was ripe to make an ass of myself.

"But fatal, *caro,* fatal. *Buona sera, Francesco. Signorina Shawn. Buona sera."* Munk and Slags moved off, Munk softly singing *Buona sera, miei signori* as they went out the door.

Clarissa had turned up a little can of red paint and a handful of brushes which she now began to pass around. I reverted to the fireplace mantel and added gin to my glass. "Try some," I said to Helen.

"Those aren't my friends," she said. "I never saw them before."

"Do you want me to make you a drink?"

"No. I'm hungry."

"I'm thirsty. Try the lobster paste."

Jonah Royal was lettering MENE MENE in red paint on the wall.

"The party's over," Helen said. "Why doesn't Clarissa let them go home?"

"I don't know about them, but I'm lonely."

Nikos was painting a life-size nude, and Mark Coulter was at work on (I) ALL MEN.

"I'm going out," said Helen. She turned abruptly, fleeing out the door into the black courtyard. I ran, caught up with her. "At least I can breathe out here," she gasped. She lingered a while, then we went down a cobbled alley and through a narrow passage to the street. We walked slowly along the street until we came to a flight of stone steps, then we climbed to the top and sat down. Helen looked beaten and empty. I unknotted my necktie, unbuttoned my shirt, and rubbed my neck. I felt dead tired myself. The street was abandoned.

"I guess it's going to stay hot all night," I said. It was an effort even to talk.

"I never thought it would end like this."

"Don't worry yourself over it," I said. "It's not your fault."

We sat in the quiet. Now and then a horn sounded and you could see headlights passing on Mount Auburn at the far end of the street. Helen's shoulder rested against mine. I took her hand—it was strangely light, almost weightless.

"Did you buy the car?" I asked.

"What?"

"The car. The other day you told me you were going to buy a car."

"Oh. That. No," she said listlessly. "It wasn't worth it. No."

I could feel the heat of Helen's arm against mine. She studied me, then she hesitantly lifted her face and let her lids fall shut—I kissed her mouth—she opened her lonely eyes and sat back. I let go of her hand.

"What do you suppose they're going to put up in there after they've taken down the house?" I asked.

"Someone said the telephone company was going to build a relay station. Whatever that is."

"It's a station with a lot of relays in it."

"Thanks," she said.

I folded my necktie slowly and neatly, and tucked it into the inside pocket of my jacket. Helen leaned back on her elbows, out of sight. There wasn't much to say.

"Will you visit me when I get settled in my new apartment?" she asked from in back of me.

"Sure. If you're good."

We talked now and again, but after a while the stone steps grew too uncomfortable to sit on, so we returned to the party in Spring Court.

Sally Kemp was sitting on the threshold of the open doorway smoking a cigarette. Nikos was gone. Mark Coulter and his roommate were gone. Almost everyone had gone home. I found my glass on the fireplace mantel; I took it to the sink and rinsed it out, then dropped in a few ice cubes. Sally Kemp wandered into the kitchen.

"Hello," she said idly. "How have you been tonight?"

"All right, I guess." I was browsing through the empty bottles on the drain board.

"Are you looking for this, by chance?" Sally held out a gin bottle.

"Thanks," I said. I made myself a drink and tasted it; it had no taste, really.

"I know all about you," Sally said.

"Oh?"

"I asked your friend Nikos. He said you're all right. A little priggish, but all right."

"That's nice. I'm glad he gave you a favorable report." I leaned back against the sink and looked at her; most of her make-up was peeling off and her hair was a mess. Her body was young, but that painted face was a real loss and made her appear old, haggard.

"What are you thinking about?" she asked.

"I don't know. Nothing, I guess."

She reached out and slid her hand inside my shirt, her palm flat on my chest. "You think you're bad off, but you don't know what bad off is," she said.

"Where's your husband?"

She shrugged and withdrew her hand. "I don't know."

I put my glass aside and we watched each other. There was only the murmur of voices from the living room.

"Want to take a walk?" I suggested. "Let's take a walk."

We slipped through the living room; then Sally hesitated at the open doorway in the dim front hall. "I don't want to go outside," she said quietly.

We drifted into the blackest corner, then I leaned back on the wall and pulled Sally against me. "Why do you wear so much make-up?" I whispered.

"Because I'm ugly."

Clarissa Cullard and Jonah Royal ran past and plunged through one of the dark doorways to a bedroom—the door slammed shut. Sally had abruptly hidden her face against mine, now I turned my head and kissed her. I began to thrust at her belly and thighs until they softly gave way; then she spread her legs and came on banging and grinding.

"Good," she muttered. "Good."

"Let's go out," I whispered. "Let's get out of here. Let's go out."

"I can't, Frank. I can't. I'm married. You know that."

I stopped and she opened her eyes, dazed. I slapped her face. She hung her head, her hair drooping down every which way.

"That's not right," she murmured. "You shouldn't do that to a friend."

I slapped her again. She backed off, her head still hanging down,

her arms limp at her sides. Someone had appeared in the front
doorway; he hesitated a moment, then walked toward us: it was
Carl Kemp. He took his wife by the hand. "Come on," he said
gently. "It's time we went home."

They vanished. I wanted to hide. I stood by the shadowy wall
for a time, then crept down the corridor. I went into the bathroom—aimed for the john bowl, pissed all over the floor, had to
mop it up with paper—washed my hands and face, and felt much
better. I was not at all sleepy and my head seemed light and clear,
as if I had been running a long time. I stepped into the corridor
and saw the closed door where Clarissa and Jonah had gone. "I
know you're in there," I crowed. "I know what you're up to." I
picked up a stray balloon and mashed it against the bedroom
door—*pow!*—then turned and walked through the hall into the living room. I rinsed out my glass, dropped in the last of the ice, then
picked up the gin bottle and returned to the others. Helen Shawn
and Dave Solomon were sitting on the floor with a man and
woman I had never seen before, and at the far end of the floor the
girl in the white dress was talking softly with a young man. Everyone else had gone home. I sat down beside Helen. They spoke in
subdued voices and laughed quietly, and I could not grasp what
the conversation was about. The young woman smiled crookedly
and said to Helen, "I ought to know. I was a mother once." Now
and again I tried to follow what they were saying, but it kept elud-
ing me. "White blood," Dave said. "It means white blood." I gave
up.

The red nude glistened on the wall; an ornate red frame had
been drawn around her and on the bottom of the frame was a
painted name-plate which said MARY MAGDALEN. Farther along the
wall there was lettering:

(1) ALL MEN ARE MORTAL
(2) MARCUS IS A MAN

Next to that was a crudely painted sickle crossed by a hammer
with *Progress!* inscribed beneath, and I noticed several lines of

strange calligraphy which looked like English script written upside down. "Is that what Pakistani looks like?" I asked. No one seemed to have heard my question. The wall with the writing on it rippled slowly, like a heavy tapestry shaken by a breeze, then it rolled smooth and was still. I studied the girl at the other end of the room: her arms were bare and golden, and she had long golden legs. I remarked about the gold color to Helen, but Helen merely smiled. I wondered what her name was. "Oh, Frank. Frank," Helen said softly.

"You think she can hear me?"

"Yes. I think she can."

"She comes from California," I whispered. "The golden state."

"Yes. You said that."

"Eureka—that's the state motto."

"That's straight gin," the young man said.

"It tastes healthy," I told him. "And it smells of pine trees. Really. Pine trees."

"What?" Helen asked.

"The gin," I said. "Here, smell it. It smells of pine trees."

"No, thanks," Helen said. She turned her head to one side and unhooked an earring, turned it the other way and removed that one, then tilted her head back and rumpled her hair. The writing on the wall wavered, the letters spreading out low and flat as if they had been painted on a rubber band. I turned away. The lamp in the corner stretched higher and slimmer, growing until it was a tall thin line; then it shrank abruptly and squatted. Now the girl was raised higher, for the room slanted up toward her and she sat at the other end of the floor as on the top edge of a tall fence, way out of reach. High thin clouds finally obscured the scene. Helen made a hole in the mist and peered in at me. I could see her entire face. She said something—I could see her lips move—but the fog was too dense for the sound to penetrate. I wondered if I was going to throw up. The floor dropped away, then Helen and Dave guided me through the dark corridor to the bathroom. The washbowl rose up, brightly lighted and gleaming with nickel and chrome, then it slid away and returned and banged my head. I heaved—my stomach caving inward, my sides collapsing, throat squeezing—heaved it all, heaved. The water swirled under my nose, soundlessly turning in the bowl around and around and around, washing away the lobster paste. Afterward I rinsed my mouth, washed my hands and face, then went to sit outside on the front doorstep. I felt awful. My guts began to clamp together like a fist.

"It was that lobster paste," I gasped. "I've been poisoned by that rotten lobster paste. It's tainted." It was getting hard to breathe.

Dave Solomon crouched down, peering at my face. "He looks all right to me," he said.

"Sure," Helen told him. "In the state you're in—"

Dave hurried away, disappeared across the dark courtyard.

"You're a doctor," I shouted. "Help me!"

"He can't help anybody," Helen muttered.

"I'm dying," I said.

A few moments later Dave returned out of the dark with a stethoscope hanging loosely about his neck. He crouched in front of me again, panting and out of breath. I unbuttoned my shirt, Dave fixed the stethoscope plugs into his ears and began to stab at my chest with the metal disk.

"I can't hear anything at all," he complained. "There's too much hair."

"Oh, God," Helen said. "You're as drunk as he is."

I was in an open car moving slowly down the street toward the river and I could not make out the driver's face. Both sides of the roadway had been leveled, black and empty, and at the far end of the street stood one narrow house. "I don't want to go home," I said. The car continued along the street and halted in front of the lone house. "Help him get to the door," Helen said. "Please help him."

I paused inside the front hall. The car motor throbbed a while, finally circled and drove up the street and dwindled away. It was silent out on the street, silent in the rooming house. I looked at Miss Cushing's disused apartment—the windows shrouded with lace, the dusty mirrors, the unlighted lamps—then I turned and started carefully on the long stairway. I mounted the first few steps, staggered, caught the rail, pulled and climbed each step, and crashed forward on the landing. A door opened overhead. "Frank?" That was Arieh Gershom. I crawled on my hands and knees, scaled the first steps, raised myself, and staggered upward. Arieh appeared, his bathrobe rushing out in a loose stream as he descended. "What happened? What happened?"

"Everyone is dying," I said.

"Let me—"

I shook him off, crawled over the top step, and rolled onto the landing between our rooms.

"What happened?" he asked.

I began to weep. "Everyone is dying."

"Who is dying?" He knelt down, put his arm beneath my shoulder, and lifted my head. "Who, Frank? Who is dying?"

"Everyone," I sobbed. "Mark Coulter. Miss Cushing. Me. You. Everyone." I went on weeping.

Arieh looked at me a while; then he gathered me to his chest and brushed my hair slowly from my eyes. "Yes," he said at last. "We are dying."

26

My full name is Frank Anthony Annunzio. My Mother once told me that when I arrived she was so gratified I was a boy that she thanked God and named me after His Saint Francis, on whose day I had been born. I was called Frank Annunzio: it was written that way in the archives of vital statistics of Boston, and after I was baptized it was added that way to the parish rolls. One autumn in Sunday school the nun asked me my middle name. I said I didn't have one. She paused and looked full at me, a pale smile on her lips. "And what will you do for a middle name on the day you are confirmed?" I said I didn't know. She slowly lowered her little roll book, closing it on one finger. "Well, now. What saint will you ask to be your patron on that day and ever afterward? What saint's name will you take?" She waited, her mild eyes peering from deep inside the white coif, the black folds of her habit hanging loose, still as an empty tent. The boys seated alongside me in the pew were turning, twisting their heads to watch. "Anthony?" I suggested. I knew nothing much about Saint Anthony, but Anthony was my father's name. "A good I-talian saint," she told us. "You pray to Saint Anthony for the recovery of lost articles." Her eyes shifted to the boy whispering behind me: "And you there,

Edward Leary. What name are you taking?" Eddie said he was going to take Patrick. "Sure now," she murmured, lifting her book.

I hated church. Saint Brendan's pews were filled with fat women who wore thick powder on their cheeks and had watery eyes, or thin shrunken women scented with eau de Cologne, younger mothers in stylish coats and fragile hats, eyes blank, overdressed children ill at ease, fretful, and a few men with faces like stones. The clustered wood columns had been painted yellow, veined and streaked to resemble tawny marble, overhead was the blue stucco blindstory and dim ceiling, and at the far end, beyond the white altar and its canopied gold tabernacle, stood the tall gray walls of the apse: a large round window of red and violet glass in the center, a painting left and right. One mural showed Mary, her hands pressed limply together, kneeling forward over the straw-filled crib in which lay the radiantly white infant Jesus; the other revealed Christ freshly risen to heaven, treading the air above a puffy cloud, the top of each bare foot slit with a pink nail hole. I was attentive when the priest unlocked the tabernacle—the little gold doors gliding open left and right, the gentle drawing out of the ciborium, the appearance of the host—but for the most part I was bored, so I used to look at the paintings and try to decide which one I disliked most. Mary's pallid face disgusted me, but so did the heart which Christ wore on his chest like some fat, rose-colored medal, a deformity crowned with thorns and sweating blood. After the last benediction the organ played "O Sacred Heart, O Sacred Heart" and we stood up, our bodies stiff and aching to move; then everyone edged clumsily into the aisles, turned to file slowly to the doors, and for a while all we could see were the tall coats in front of us. Outside the sun was so bright it hurt your eyes, and the air was as fresh as cold water, good to the face; from the top step you could see the oval curve of the gravel drive, the empty trees, and beneath them the cars parked along both sides of the street. Sunday school was gathering downstairs in the lower church, but we lingered outside and fooled around and only at last charged the door, cramming ourselves down the worn stairway, dunking our fingers in the stoup *In the Name of the Father and the Son and Holy Ghost,* flicking holy water at each other as we broke through the padded swinging door—girls to the left, boys to the right—clattering the knee-benches and filling the pews with an echoing hubbub as a dozen different classes began to recite their lessons at once. The cate-chism was a little book with a pale blue paper cover:

> Q. Who made you?
> A. God made me.
>
> Q. Who is God?
> A. God is the Creator of heaven and earth, and of all things.
>
> Q. What is man?
> A. Man is a creature composed of body and soul, and made

to the image and likeness of God.

We learned about sin, the Ten Commandments, the Seven Sacra-ments, the Four Last Things, and the Virgin Mary. The greatest puzzle was Mary, Mother of God. In the beginning there was only God, then God made the world and down on the world He planted a paradise, and from the wet earth of that paradise He made Adam, and from Adam's rib made Eve, so they were both naked, the man and his wife in the garden, and they were not ashamed. I guessed what early delight it had been for them, walking naked in the garden of pleasure and not ashamed. It seemed to have been like my grandparents' garden in Sicily, the garden so heavy with figs and oranges that the tree limbs bent, split, and fell with their loads, where you rested in the woven shade of the grape arbor and drank cold water from the spring, the garden where my mother had strolled when she was a girl, and I knew what paradise it would be to walk out under that hot sun, naked but not ashamed. Later the serpent tempted Eve to eat the fruit of the tree of knowl-edge, which God had forbidden to them, and when she had eaten she tempted Adam, and after they both had eaten they grew ashamed of their nakedness and put on fig leaves; then God caught them and for their disobedience expelled them from the garden, doomed them to sickness and death. Our nature was corrupted by the sin of our first parents, which darkened our understanding, weakened our will, and left in us a strong inclination to evil. The sin which we inherit from our first parents is called original sin.

Q. Does this corruption of our nature remain in us after original sin is forgiven?

A. This corruption of our nature and other punishments remain in us after original sin is forgiven.

Eve succumbed to the risen serpent, fell to the imperial thoughts swelling his proud flesh, tasted the forbidden fruit, and, with her lips still wet, turned to Adam and offered her taste to him, yielding and drawing him down to her, embracing him and enrapturing all men forever, luring all mankind downward to that feast. God punished Eve, gave her pain in childbirth where there would have been no pain before, punished all women after her but Mary. Mary, in her Immaculate Conception, was preserved from original sin and born spotless: her flesh ever pure, the leaved openings of her body shining as the golden doors of the canopied tabernacle, her womb the ciborium into which God poured His Son in the fiery stream of the Holy Ghost as easily as the priest pours wine into a chalice, her womb the chalice from which was taken nine months later the infant Jesus, leaving Mary still and forever virgin. Now her statue brooded at the altar rail—Virgin Mary, Mother of Jesus, Mother of God, Queen of Heaven—half hooded, wrapped in blue, mild yet austere and reproachful.

After reciting our lessons we could ask questions. Boyle asked did you have to use holy water in baptism, or could you use faucet water from the kitchen. Sister Brigid told him you could use any sort of water from any place, so long as it was water. Then Eddie and someone began giggling, and Eddie asked if you could use spit. Sister Brigid sent him to the altar rail to say ten Our Fathers. I asked Sister why we had to go to confession once a month, even when we thought we had not sinned.

"Only a saint never sins. Boys sin all the time. They can't help it." She smiled cheerfully, her eyes peeping at me. "And who was born without sin?" she asked.

"The Blessed Virgin Mary. But what happens if you sin and then die before you get ready to go to confession?" I asked.

"You go to hell," Dan said loudly.

"Oh?" Sister Brigid said, turning to him. "Do you now?" She opened her eyes very wide and leaned back, exaggerating her surprise. "And can you tell me how many kinds of actual sin there are?"

Dan hesitated, grew cautious. "Mortal and venial," he said tentatively.

"What happens if you have committed only venial sins?" she asked him.

"Then you go to purgatory," I volunteered.

"Who can name me some mortal sins?" she asked.

"Murder is a mortal sin," Boyle said. "Or missing Mass on Sunday. Or not believing in God."

"And if you die with a mortal sin on your soul?" she asked. "What then?"

"Then you are damned and you go to hell," Dan cried. He grinned at us, for he liked to say *hell* and *damn* and get away with it.

"For how long?" Sister Brigid poked her rolled-up catechism over my head at the boys in back. "For how long?"

"Forever," Maloney said promptly. "For all eternity."

We went to confession on the first Friday of every month, between three and five o'clock in the afternoon. At that hour the lower church was a quiet dim space lighted only by the amber windows just below the ceiling. At the far end there was a low altar rail and two pyramids of vigil lights, the flames on the melted wax glowing ruby or ultramarine deep within their little glass cups; behind the rail, as if dug into the back wall of a cave, there was a dark altar covered with a white scarf and surmounted by a carved oak altarpiece, a rank of thin saints standing in pendulous triple-arched niches like sentries. The confessional was a narrow booth flanked by curtained alcoves; the priest sat behind the center door and we entered on either side—girls to the left, boys to the right. I seated myself in one of the pews and tried to think of some sins I had committed. The pew in front of me had two boys in it, the one in front of that had five, and the first couple were empty. On the other side of the aisle the girls were perched together in the front two rows. A few of the girls had hats, but most were wearing kerchiefs knotted under the chin, and one fat girl who had forgotten to bring anything at all had covered her head with a small white handkerchief held in place by a pink hair clip. My attention kept turning away from sins, and when I forced it back my mind went blank. I felt bored and listless and wished I were someplace else, but I kept at it until I had three sins—I had missed Mass one Sunday, I had given way to anger, I had yielded to sloth. I hunched forward in the confessional, knelt on the low step with my arms resting on the sill beneath the closed panel. The air was rancid, heavy with the odor of candle wax and wood polish, cigar smoke, damp cloth. On the back wall there was a broken crucifix: a tack had fallen from Christ's palm and a length of plaster had dropped from his shin, exposing the wire armature of his leg. I heard a blurred murmur, a rattle, then footsteps went past. The panel slid open and on the other side the priest shifted his weight, leaned sideways toward me from the shadow, his face sunk behind his dim hand, the bulk of his shoulder. The odor of cigar smoke came more strongly: it was old Father O'Shea.

"Bless me, Father, for I have sinned."

"When was the last time you came to confession?" He coughed, coughed again, and cleared his throat.

"The first Friday of last month."

"Is that you, Frank?"

"Yes."

"Ah. And how's your mother?"

"She's fine."

"That's good. Good. Do you hear much from your grandfather these days?" He used to share grandfather's best wine and best cigars, my mother said, and grandfather used to call him Mr O'Shea.

"No," I said. "Not much. We get two letters a year."

"Ah, well, the war. Ah. Let's see. You've been to Mass every Sunday?"

"I missed one Sunday. I got up late. I mean I was lazy."

"Any swearing or cursing?"

"No."

"Disobey your parents?"

"Once or twice. Once in a while, I guess."

"Get angry with them? Lose your temper? Sometimes?"

"Yes."

"Steal anything?"

"No."

"Lie? Cheat?"

"No. No."

"Impure thoughts?"

I hesitated, reluctant. "Yes."

"Do you dislike them?" he suggested. "Try to think of other things? Banish them?"

"Yes," I murmured. I wondered if I were lying.

"Do you say your morning and evening prayers? Or do you forget? Now and then?"

"I forget, now and then."

"Well, now. Say five Our Fathers and five Hail Marys, and be a good boy."

"Yes, Father."

I began *O my God I am heartily sorry* against the swift whispering murmur of Father O'Shea's Latin, and as we finished the panel slid rattling shut. I stepped from the confessional with lowered eyes and went to the near corner of the altar rail to say my penance. The Virgin stood on a pedestal so close by my shoulder that I could reach out and touch her toes. The dusty blue folds of plaster cloth made a tight cowl about her head, hung stiffly from her shoulders straight to her ankles, and she gazed down upon me with heavy-lidded eyes, a faint smile. Just below the hem of her robe I could see a thick snake, its glistening purple blunt-fleshed head imprisoned beneath the gentle weight of her small bare foot. I laid my fists on the rail and said the prayers, unfolding one finger of my right hand for each Our Father, and one finger of my left for each Hail Mary.

On Confirmation Day we filed from our pews in the lower church, went outside and up the stairs to the big double doors under the middle arch, then bumped each other up the center aisle to our new seats, girls to the left and boys to the right. The bishop stood before the altar rail flanked by Father Mooney and Father O'Shea. The bishop was tall, massive, had a face as lumpy and hard as a rock potato: "Now I am going to ask you a few questions." His voice boomed and rattled. "Today you come of age spiritually and become soldiers of Christ. You enroll in the army of Our Lord. But before you march up here to receive the sacrament and welcome the Holy Ghost into your souls, I want you to show me—and show your proud parents and relatives and friends gathered here—how well you know your faith. Don't be shy, now." He rested his hand upon his stomach, his thumb and forefinger lightly pinching the base of his pectoral cross; then he descended the step and began to stroll slowly down the aisle, his robes moving heavily. Father Mooney and Father O'Shea followed one pace behind him. "Now, who can name the Seven Sacraments for me?" He halted and turned his head left and right, a thin smile chiseled on his face. Father Mooney lowered his eyes, but old Father O'Shea smiled encouragingly at one of the girls and she raised her hand. "Yes?" the Bishop asked. The girl recited the Seven Sacraments. The bishop turned toward us. "And who can tell me about baptism? Can the rite of baptism be performed only by a priest?" Father O'Shea looked mildly surprised, then shook his head as if in disbelief. "Can it be performed by a layman?" asked the bishop. Father O'Shea brightened, nodding his head in agreement. One of the boys in back of me answered yes. "Good. Good. We're off to a good start," the Bishop said. Later we knelt at the altar rail, and the Bishop came with the priests to each of us—placed a hand on my head, anointed my forehead with holy chrism in the form of a cross, then laid his warm hand against my cheek, giving me that symbolic blow to put me in mind that I must be ready to suffer anything, even death, for the sake of Christ. Afterward we marched out through the church doors into the sunshine, descending the church steps and spreading out onto the grass oval inside the gravel drive. It looked like a party to see us standing on the lawn so dressed up and not moving much for fear of mussing our clothes: we wore dark suits and our neckties were red, the girls' ribbons were red, to symbolize those tongues of fire in which the Holy Ghost appeared to the apostles. The bishop and old Father O'Shea swapped jokes while Father Mooney and the nuns hung back in a semicircle, listening politely and smiling. Now and again one of the girls went up to the Bishop with her parents and called him Your Excellency—Peggy Timothy even kissed his ring—and he let anyone stand beside him and pose for a photo. My father had gone to look for Ed and Mary; my mother and Dan's mother were standing together, talking. "Aren't we all fine and dandy today," Dan's mother said, looking over at us. My mother smiled. "Frank, dear, leave your necktie alone," she said. Dan and I moved off, circling around until we were on the edges of the crowd where the people were shaking hands, saying good-by, walking slowly down the street to their cars. So I unbuttoned my collar and pulled off my red necktie, and stuffed it into the inner pocket of my jacket.

27

THIS PAGE
for
TIMOTHY STEWART

Best of roommates, who let me share his apartment
on Boylston Street one summer, who woke early and
dressed quietly and always left fresh coffee in the
pot, and who gave me the iron bedspring with which
I set up housekeeping in an apartment of my own.

Drowned Off Fire Island
Aet. XXVIII

28

Beth was the most dazzling woman I had ever seen. She was built. I first met her the day I moved into the Mount Auburn Street apartment. I was coming down the street with my iron bedspring—hauling it under one arm until it tore my shoulder apart, tucking it under the other arm a while, hoisting it overhead in both hands—and when I sighted her she was in a tight white jersey and tight red shorts, crouched on the sidewalk washing the basement windows, her chromium-blond hair glittering in the sun. "You just move in?" I asked her.

"Yes." She smiled and stood up. Oh, she was beautifully put together, all right.

"Would you like to see my apartment?" she asked.

"Sure," I said.

She had painted the walls white and the cement floor a reddish shade of brown; the wall over the sink was hung with copper-bottomed pans, the open shelves were stacked with bright dishes and glassware, she had a lot of furniture made of steel and canvas, a big television set in the corner, and a large ugly painting propped against the wall. "I'm from Michigan and haven't talked to anybody since I got here. I don't know a soul. But I like it," she said lightly.

"You don't know anyone at all?"

"Oh." She shrugged and tilted her head. "Oh, I have a job. I begin work next week. I'll meet people, I guess. If I want to," she amended.

"Divorced?"

"In about two weeks," she said.

I told her my name. "If you need anything, let me know."

"Are you sure?"

"Sure I'm sure."

I met her next time at Communications Control—CoCo on Route 128—when Scott and I were out there on a business visit. One of their young men did all the talking and when the lecture was over Scott and the CoCo people went on a tour of the building while I stayed behind, presumably to amplify and arrange my notes. I collected my papers and put them in the brief case and looked around, then looked through the glass wall at the young woman in the next office. She was seated amid a tangle of electrical cord, her calm empty face toward me and her eyes blank as light bulbs; her foot tapped a pedal and her fingers hovered, flashed, went driving over the keys of a typewriter. One cord ran from under her foot up to the gray dictating box at her side, a jack from the box was plugged in her ear, another cable descended from the typewriter and curled into the scrawl of telephone and intercom lines beneath her desk—the girl in the middle of the circuit was the one who had moved into the basement apartment. I walked down the hall and into her office just as she had replaced the phone and was turning to the typewriter. She smiled, kicked aside the pedal and pulled the plug from her ear and pressed a tab on the humming typewriter. The room was silent. "What's your name?" I asked her. "You never told me."

"Beth Wright."

"Is that the old name?"

"It's my new name, the name I was born with."

"Are you busy tonight?"

"No," she said. "Do you want to come down?"

That evening when Beth ushered me into her apartment she was dressed in a white terry-cloth bathrobe. "Do you mind if I take a bath?" she asked.

"I'm sorry. I didn't realize I was early."

"You're not. You're right on time. I just want to take a bath," she explained. "Turn on the TV," she said briskly. "Some good shows tonight."

She slipped into the bathroom and pulled the door firmly shut. I turned on the TV. A while later I heard water draining from the tub and Beth came out wrapped in her robe, vanished into the next room, then returned in a tight pair of pale blue trousers and a stiff white blouse. I turned off the TV.

"Would you like to go out?" I suggested.

"I thought we might stay here and have some coffee." She lit the gas under the pot, took a couple of cups from the shelf. "What do you do for a living?"

"I work for someone named Scott at Research/Research."

"Are you an engineer?"

"I'm a technical writer."

"Oh." She sounded faintly disappointed.

I told her I was also an unsuccessful painter.

"What do you think of that one?" She glanced toward the big ugly canvas which hung on the wall above the divan.

"Well," I said hesitantly. I peered at it, hunting for a signature, afraid that she might have painted it herself. "It has a lot of technique."

"My ex-husband did that. He was a painter."

"Why don't you take it down?" I asked her. "I should think it would remind you of him."

She shrugged. "It's such a bare-ass wall otherwise."

So I sat on the divan and watched her pour the coffee. Her face was so clear and smooth that it looked polished. We drank in silence a few moments, then she leapt from her chair and returned with a long envelope from which she drew a folded sheet of stiff paper. "My divorce," she said crisply, handing me the paper. It was a fancy legal announcement which began with wildly scrolled Gothic characters, descended into a paragraph of Roman type, and concluded with a gilt paper sunburst glued beneath the last line. "No alimony," she said. "I come free and clear."

"It looks fake," I said, laughing.

"I know. But it's really real. The lawyer sent it to me." She smiled. "Only the marriage was a fake."

I handed her back the document. She studied it with a satisfied smile, then she refolded it, inserted it carefully into the envelope, and returned it to the cabinet. I was at one end of the divan and now she seated herself at the other end.

"Well, you know all there is to know about me," she said. She sprang up and crossed the room. "I know what. We can look at TV. There's some good shows tonight."

I groaned.

"Don't you like television?"

"Sure, sure," I said hastily. "Turn it on."

Beth crouched by the set, switching from scene to scene until she found a Western; then she stood up and drew to one side to gaze at it. She sucked in her stomach and pushed the loosened folds of her blouse into her pants, pulling and tucking until her breasts drove like spikes against the starched cloth. At length she turned off all the lights except the lamp on the cabinet, came and sat at the far end of the divan, and pulled her legs up, folding them between us. We watched the screen, remarking now and again on the action, until the hour passed and the drama finished. "More coffee?" Beth asked, standing.

"It's time for me to go home to bed." I was getting sullen.

"I notice you walking everywhere," she said, ignoring my last remark. "Don't you own a car?"

"No. I don't own a car."

"You don't own a car?" She was amazed.

"I like to walk."

Beth went to the cabinet, reached into a bowl, and fished out a short beaded chain with some keys on it. "Here," she said, coming across the room. "I have an extra set of car keys. Take them."

"No, thanks."

"Why not?" She tossed the loop of keys to me and I automatically caught them.

"I don't need your car."

"Keep them for a while. The two little ones are for the car. The big key is for the apartment." She went to the stove to heat the coffee.

"Beth, I don't want them."

"Please. Just keep them for a while. All right?" She looked at me a moment, pleading. "See what you can find on TV," she suggested.

We watched the screen for another hour; then I stood up and said good night, and went back upstairs to my apartment.

Beth Wright came out of Willow Run where she had been secretary to an automobile executive, was twenty-five years old, and had been married six years to an abstract painter, and was now divorced. She had weighed 120 pounds twice in her life: on the day she married and the day she split. Beth told me those few little facts, and that was about all she said about herself. She never spoke of anything in her past or in any past, but carried on as if her splendid body had been put together whole, without growth or memory, and sent FOB to Cambridge. She had thick platinum hair, short and glittering, a clear face, and a medium frame with rather long legs and firm, golden-hued flesh. It was a well-made body and she treated it with care, kept it up. I have seen her an hour at one fingernail—removing the old lacquer, cutting back the cuticle, trimming, sanding, polishing, painting—not for vanity, but because she had beautifully articulated hands which gave her joy to work on. She wore almost no make-up, never any perfume save the faint odor of her bath soap, and when she emerged from the tub her skin was illuminated by the scrubbing she had given it. "Watch this," she would say, tightening her bathrobe sash—then she would fling her hands down, touch the carpet with her palms, spring up—"And I never bent my knees!" She had cereal for breakfast, ate a thin sandwich and drank a glass of milk for lunch, and for dinner took a shallow bowl of soup or a salad leaf. I never knew how she kept alive. In the beginning I used to ask her out to dinner, but she always said that she had just finished eating (a cup of chowder, a spoonful of cottage cheese on lettuce), said she didn't feel hungry at all. She was forever on the move—rising from her chair to turn on the TV, smoothing a ripple in the carpet with her foot, sorting quickly through a stack of phonograph records, tossing a burnt match into the sink, crossing the floor to switch off a light, landing for a moment beside me on the divan, then taxiing down the room to take flight again. Yet there was rarely anything anxious or agitated in her: she simply enjoyed moving.

The only thing that could bring Beth down was a bout of poor health. One evening she looked awful—her face puffy, with brown shadows under the eyes—and she insisted that she felt fine, really, but she thought she needed to rest, needed to get to bed, needed a little sleep. "I'll phone you in a day or two," she added. Yet she didn't phone, so a couple of days later I phoned her and when she didn't answer I went around outside, unlocked the door, and let myself in. She was laid out on the divan under a blanket, asleep, with some soiled dishes on the floor beside her. I roused her, asked her how she was feeling. "Much better," she whispered. I asked why didn't she call a doctor. "I don't know any doctors." I told her I would give her the name of a doctor. "I don't need any doctors," she said weakly. "I'm not ready for the scrap heap yet." I washed the dishes, peered into the refrigerator, and asked her did she want me to buy her any food, anything at all, anything. She said that all she wanted was some ginger ale and a TV guide and maybe a magazine. I asked her if she owned a thermometer. "No," she said. I left and came back with the ginger ale, a TV guide, three glossy magazines, and a thermometer. Her temperature was down close to normal. "I told you I was feeling better," she said triumphantly.

But most of that autumn Beth was in tiptop shape. She bought a yellow kitten and a row of green plants, and no matter how late she invited me down to visit she was apt to take a bath. Some evenings I would find her at the ironing board, clad in a pale slip, a fragile blouse in one hand and a glittering steam iron in the other. "Do you mind if I go on ironing?" she used to ask. "I only have a little more to do." So far as I could see, Beth was never wearing anything under her slip, but she seemed absolutely indifferent to my presence. So I would look at the television screen and she would slowly work her way through her collection of fragmentary garments—half-slips, strapless bras, abbreviated vests, sleeveless blouses, dickeys, backless sundresses. One evening I came at her invitation and entered to find her at the ironing board in a bra and underpants. "For God's sake!" I said. She licked her middle finger and tapped it against the sizzling iron to test for heat, ignoring me. "I'll be through in a little bit. Can't you wait?" she asked. I took the kitten from the divan and sat down; the kitten was bigger now, and when it tried to sink those needle teeth into my hand it hurt. "Have you named this animal yet?" I asked. Beth picked up a long bottle and began sprinkling water over one of the undergarments. "I call it pussycat," she said, studying her handiwork. I asked if the name was male or female. "Female," she said. "And that reminds me, I'll have to have her fixed soon."

Beth's face was a pleasure to look at. It did not stun you, did not stab you in the guts and drain your heart: in a way it was plain, open, and blank, almost like a mirror which can reflect any configuration or depth but which is itself mere polished surface. Her body was a seamless ideal, the pattern beyond all women, that limiting figure toward which all female measurements converge. Yet it too did not terrify with beauty, or even surprise you after a while. Past the first few moments of seeing Beth you came to a sense of familiarity about her, as if what you saw were what you remembered from someplace else, somebody else, and in time you might realize that she was so recognizable because a hundred versions of her appeared each week on magazine covers and advertisements, calendars, pin-ups, movie stills, fashion plates. The dazzlement you felt on seeing her the first time was the shock of finding the flat projection of fantasy incarnate and rounded in the sun. Now, I never saw Beth except at night in her basement apartment, buried six feet underground, illuminated by lamp light or the blue glow from the television screen, and half of me was beginning to doubt that she was real. And I had never touched her. I don't know why. Perhaps it was because I had come to believe in her solely as an image and not something to be grabbed at; or maybe her indifference to my presence as she shed her garments piece by piece over the weeks, less and less aware of me, had led me to believe that I was disembodied, not really there at all. At night now I would lie in my bed picturing how I should go about it—grab her by the wrist, whirling, wrenching the last flimsy bra and panties from her (yank, rip, toss it aside) fling her to the carpet—but each evening the proper moment never ripened and I would have to return, climb back upstairs to my flat, and try to sleep. One morning I awoke cold, terrified with guilt, went to my kitchen window and stared out at the cinder courtyard, kept watch over Beth's parked car until she emerged from her apartment and drove off to work: then I crept back to bed, relieved that I had not murdered her in my sleep. The following morning was the same, and the next also the same. So on Friday evening I took Beth's keys from the hook in my kitchen, walked into her living room, and said, "Here. Take them back. In one more week you'll be naked and I'll be blind from looking at TV." Beth gave me a blank stare. "Let's go for a ride," she said suddenly. "And you drive." That's the way it all started.

29

Beth owned a new car, small and neat and shaped like a shoe box, with a sturdy engine, a tight wheel, stiff action, and firm springs. She knotted a silk scarf around her neck and I drove us to the river, headed upstream on Route 3, and then pulled away on 2, working through the bright confusion of discount stores, gas stations, doughnut stands, until we lifted over Belmont Hill and dropped into the dark. "I take this road every morning," Beth said. "Where do you suppose it goes?" I told her it went to the western end of Massachusetts. "Let's not," she said. So when we hit Route 128 I swung in and turned south. Beth switched on the radio and found some light music, then leaned back and relaxed. "I like this. I like driving in the dark," she murmured later. We followed the sweep of 128 through the wooded countryside, moving south and curving gently eastward more and more. It was pleasant to drive a car, I had forgotten how much I enjoyed it. Beth was still, tranquil, languid. We cut through the Blue Hills and instead of curving up north to Boston I kept going, shot off 128 into a labyrinth of flashing yellow lights, detour signs, arrows, bumped up onto a narrow road and came to a halt under a sign: PLYMOUTH 30 MI. "Let's go to Plymouth Rock," she suggested. About an hour later we rounded into a small town and spotted a road sign which pointed the way to the beach, came onto the shore road, and ran down to Plymouth. I parked the car and we walked over to the sea wall. The site was deserted—a square stone roof, an iron cage, the rock itself amid a dark shoal of pebbles. "Now let's go home," she said. We drove back on Route 3, turned on 128 for a while, then headed into the city on 16 and rolled into Cambridge sometime after midnight. It had been a pleasant little ride. I was feeling good and Beth looked happy, almost excited. She ducked down to her apartment and I went up to my door, reached in my pocket, and discovered that I did not have my key. I had locked myself out. That's a fact. I stood in the silent hallway and thought about waking up the janitor, then decided not to try it. I want around and knocked on Beth's door. "I forgot my apartment key," I said. She shrugged. "Come in. I'm going to bed." She disappeared into her bedroom. I hesitated, took off my jacket and laid it over the back of a chair, then sat on the sofa and tried to think what I was doing. Beth reappeared in her white robe, carrying a fresh towel and face cloth, new soap. She set them on the end of the divan. "If you want to wash up," she explained. She slipped into the bathroom, came out a short while later, vanished into her room. I took off my shirt, washed, returned to the divan, and started to undress, got stripped down to the waist and bare feet. Beth appeared: "Are you going to sleep out here, or in the bedroom? It's a big enough bed," she added. The bedroom was painted white and the bureau was bare except for a large framed photograph of a man's face, a pair of hard eyes and the top of his head like an upturned hairbrush. I asked who he was. "Just a friend," she said. The kitten shot from under the bed and pounced at my bare feet—Beth scooped her up and bowled her through the doorway, shut the door. "Don't you want to put away the photo?" I suggested. Beth glanced at it, then shrugged. "No," she said lightly. She walked to the far side of the bed and turned on the small table lamp. The bed was big, all right. It was immense. The bedspread had a pattern of black and white diamonds, distorted and irregular, which gave it the long perspective of a grand uncompleted crossword puzzle, a vast checkerboard, a public square. I sank my fingers tentatively into the bed. "It feels odd," I said. "It feels like—" Beth furled the bedspread. "I know," she said. "It's foamy rubber. It's marvelous. Now hurry." I unbuckled my pants and had started to fold them across the chair when the loose change struck—nickels, dimes, quarters, half-dollars, cascading pennies, bouncing and ringing, wheeling around this way and that, circling under the chair and bed, rolling across the dim floor. Beth snapped off the overhead light, cast aside her pale robe and dove onto the bed. "Oh, hell, hurry it up," she said. But I was not much good that night.

I did not see Beth for a week, then on Friday evening we hopped into her car and drove off again. I headed out along Route 2— "Let's go all the way to the end," she said—did not turn north or south but flew across 128 and kept going. "I helped pour the concrete for that overpass back there," I told her. "Is that so?" she replied, uninterested. She leaned forward and turned on the radio, began hunting for music. We passed the lights of Concord, then the road opened wide into the dark and I stepped on the gas. Now the music was coming in soft and clear and Beth had settled back, contented. The tires hummed. I could feel the rising grade of the road; it was not much, but it was there and we were riding it. The air was clear, cool. "It's a great night for driving," I said. Beth let her eyes close: "I could go on like this forever, forever," she murmured. Later the music began to drift and sink—Beth touched the knob, turning it slightly—the music grew and remained clear for a while, then it wavered and shrank, disappeared. "That's the last of Boston," I said. She stirred herself, lit a cigarette, began hunting across the dial for a local station. We mounted the long, shallow hills, dropping now and again, but always rising higher. The road narrowed, slowed, turned through the little towns of Gardner and Templeton; then the lights scattered and vanished and we lifted into the dark, and later again we dipped, twisted along a stream past Erving, soared over the Connecticut River, and from there curved down through a patch of houses and came rolling into the town of Greenfield. Here we paused for coffee (Beth, sleepy and flushed, drained her cup and tapped her long nails on the counter: "Let's get going. Let's go."), then continued out the main street into the dark and rode the steep curving highway up toward the Berkshires. The music had dwindled to a hum. Beth turned the knob, caught a local station and then lost it, found another, but a short time later the music had vanished. She sighed, turned it off. Later she gazed past me at the black, tumbling Deerfield River. "Is this still Route 2?" she asked. I told her it was. "It's weird," she said. I asked her did she want me to tell her about the Deerfield massacre. She said no. "The Indians crept up with the wind," I said. "Every time the wind blew it rustled the leaves and the Indians ran in closer. The settlers never heard them until too late." We cruised along the Mohawk Trail, passed over the Cold River, and kept moving higher—shifted to second—upward to the Eastern Summit and Whitcomb Summit—shifted to third and rolled to a stop at the top of the hairpin. We got out of the car, went past a low dark building, and walked out onto an observation deck. The wood planks made a hollow sound beneath our shoes and the wind was chill. "Here we are," I said. Beth went to the rail and looked down into the steep valley where a sprinkling of lights still glowed. "That's Massachusetts," I told her. "Over there is New York, and up that way is Vermont." A car moved past us down the mountain, and we watched its headlights vanish, then reappear below, and finally sweep from sight under the black trees. "Let's go," Beth said. We swung into the valley, cruised through Williamstown, and rode along until we came to the last motel in the state. It was almost midnight. I registered, laid the money on the counter, and as soon as we were inside our room Beth stripped off her clothes, stepped into the bathroom, and shut the door. A few moments later I heard the drumming rush of shower water. I undressed slowly and lay on the bed, rather tired. After a while the shower noise stopped and Beth appeared, her brilliant flesh quivering with water drops and her eyes sparkling. "Hurry it up. I'll show you something new," she said. Beth murmured and purred in the shadowy room, and even when it seemed that she must be silent—her eyes clamped shut, her mouth open without breath—I could hear yet within her a deep, soft, endless humming. Afterward I felt half dead. She lay beside me with her eyes lidded, her seamless body aglow and cooling, while I stared up at the gray plaster. Then she stirred, rolled from the bed, padded across the floor, and threw the overhead light on. "Let's hit the road, Frank. I want to wake up in my own apartment." My God, I was tired.

I did not see Beth at all during the next week; then on Friday evening I went down to her apartment and she said, "Let's try going the other way. Maybe it will work better." So we slid into the car, pulled onto Route 2, and headed downstream into Boston. While we were crossing the Charles into the city I asked her how far she wanted to go this time. "All the way," she said. I told her that Route 2 came to its end in a few more miles. "Oh? Well, I want to go to the end of the map, Cape Cod." We ground through the city for a couple of blocks, then I turned and wheeled slowly onto Storrow Drive and began moving, rolled along gathering more and more speed, thundered up the ramp to the expressway, stepped on the gas, and took off, airborne. The sky was black, but the buildings beneath us seemed to be standing in a sea of light. "One of my grandfathers owned a store down there," I said. Beth smiled, leaned back, shut her eyes: "I like this. I really like this." We crossed over the North End, banked past the Custom House Tower and over India Street toward the Fort Point Channel, turned still more and began descending, dropped gently down to street level, plunged underground for a few blocks, and finally lifted to the surface of the broad roadway leading from the city to the Cape. A while later we slid over, merged onto Route 3, and traveled through the flat land along the coast, raced past Plymouth and kept edging closer to the shore, glimpsed the lights standing ahead high over the canal, slowed up over the Bourne Bridge and down, dropping between the dark grassy walls of the highway to shoot blindly through Sandwich, Barnstable, Yarmouth, Dennis, Harwich, Brewster, and Orleans, then out to the open road gray now with boarded-up ice-cream stands and shadowy clamburger booths, passing by the darkened motels of Eastham, North Eastham, Wellfleet, through Truro to the lights of Provincetown. I started to slow a bit. "It's midnight. Let's get off the road and into a motel," I suggested. Beth turned on me, alarmed. "Don't stop *now*," she cried. "We're not at the end yet!" So I veered around Provincetown, put on a final burst of speed and kept it up until we hit Race Point, then pulled from the highway and coasted across an empty parking lot, rolling to a stop at last. I felt tired, beat. "That's all there is," I told her. Beth leaned forward, squinting at the pale sand field and the stumpy platform, the black ocean. We got out—there was a stiff breeze, the air was cold, damp. She mounted the low observation deck but the flying sand stung her legs, made her cringe back to the leeward side of the car, gasping. She shivered, her eyes watery: "Find us a motel. Quick. I want a hot shower." I found a place and undressed, lay on the bed half asleep until Beth emerged from the bathroom, her flesh steaming in the cool gray air—"Let's try a different way," she whispered. I was not so good that night and any which way we went at it made no difference. Afterward Beth lay beside me in the chill room, humming slower and slower as she caught her breath; then she tumbled from the bed and I drove us back to Cambridge. The next Friday we hopped onto US Route 1 and barreled southward into Rhode Island, churned through Providence, kept going southward on new segments of Interstate 95 and then westerly into Connecticut, and pushing—Beth wanted it—pushing toward Greenwich, pushing on down that long toll road into the dark so that gradually I lost all sense of riding anywhere, saw only the smooth highway sliding beneath me, and heard only the steady murmurous purring of the tires until I was dizzy, or tired, or so bored that I finally gave it up, pulled out, and we rolled to a stop at Stratford. A week later we cut northwestward through New Hampshire into Vermont and joined US 5, aiming for Burlington, but I made it only to a cold room at White River Junction.

The following Friday night we laid onto Interstate 95 and headed for Maine. I asked Beth how far she wanted to go. "Bar Harbor," she said. I told her we would never make it that far. "We will if you drive fast enough. I'm willing to try anything. So let's try it," she said. It was a black night, the road was wide open, and we pounded away, making time. As we approached Portland we ran into a thin mist and then a drizzle. I turned on the windshield wipers, kept up the speed. We skimmed through Portland, came to some unfinished segments of 95, slanted over to US 1 and passed through Bath. It had begun to rain; the roadway glistened and the light from our headlamps was unable to catch on anything, so I slowed down. After Camden the rain thinned and grew softer, began to cling momentarily to the windshield, and as we came into Belfast I noticed that the sides of the road were pale. "It's crazy but it's snowing," Beth said. It was long after midnight when we crossed the Penobscot. We rolled on through Ellsworth, then I turned toward the shore and a while later pulled from the road and came to a stop somewhere at the edge of the sea. "I've had it," I said. "I quit." We crept out of the car to look around; the air was cool and damp, the snowflakes swimming gently in the beam of the headlamps melted as they touched the black roadway. I leaned back against the door and turned my face up to the falling snow, opened my mouth. "Isn't this stuff radioactive?" Beth asked. "It doesn't matter that much," I said. She moved away and stood gazing into the dark toward the sea for a while, then she returned. "Let's skip the motel and go back home now," I suggested. "All right," she said lightly. It was a pleasant ride home, the best. I cruised along the empty highway at my own speed; Beth turned the radio, smoked, talked now and again. It had stopped snowing when we passed through Belfast, and south from Camden the road was dry. We picked up WBAL in Baltimore for a time. It came in clear and we listened to their music, a forecast of their distant weather conditions, and then more music until it faded off the dial. Beth told me about her job and about one of the other secretaries whom she liked. I cut off the highway in Portland and we found an all-night diner where we ate scrambled eggs. While we were finishing our coffee Beth studied her fingernail polish: "I wish I could keep my life as neat as I keep my hands," she said. The air was biting cold when we walked back to the car. Beth took the wheel from Portland to Kittery while I dozed in the corner, then she slept and I continued on through Boston and into Cambridge. I shook her shoulder: "It's daylight. Wake up." She waited drowsily while I unlocked the door to her apartment, then I guided her down into the shaded living room and asked her if she was going to be all right. She sat on the edge of the divan, drew up her legs and curled over on her side, asleep. I walked her into the bedroom and she began at last to undress, dropping her garments weakly on the floor. Two pennies were taped to the wall above the bureau. "What are these for?" I asked her. She looked over, heavy-lidded: "Do you want those back?" She made a slight, feeble gesture and slid heavily beneath the bedcovers. I turned off the lamp, went out pulling the door shut behind me so it locked, then walked around to my apartment and went to bed.

30

After that I stopped seeing Beth. At Christmastime I went home and celebrated the holidays with my parents and brother and sister, our uncles and aunts and cousins; it was good to see family again. Scott and I had discovered that we worked well together, and although I did not plan to spend my life at Research/Research I enjoyed going to the office in the morning, talking with Marian Malone, drinking coffee with Ibera and his crew across the hall. I had free time and energy and I was painting well: I figured that in six more months I might have enough good canvas for a small show. I went to the movies every so often with Fitzpatrick or Saltares, and about once a week Nikos walked over to my place or I walked over to his. Helen Shawn gave me a Christmas present; I had said something about always having wanted to own a pair of fur-lined gloves, so she gave me a pair—took me by surprise. On those gray Sunday mornings I would buy a *Times* and stroll over to her apartment for breakfast; now and again I took her out to dinner, or she asked me to escort her some place, or we spent an evening in her tiny living room playing a game of chess. Early that spring someone told me that Michelle had married Ralph Bretton; I had met him once at a party, but could not remember much else about him. Later I bumped into Michelle in the Square and she told me about her marriage, asked me to come visit her sometime, any time. I said yes, and let it slip my mind. Then we ran into each other in the Square another noon and she invited me again, so I telephoned her that evening and she said she was alone but come over, please come over. The house was tucked away in a little park behind Tory Road.

"I never knew this street existed," I told her.

Michelle smiled briefly. "Rich people know about it. Come in. Let me take your raincoat."

The living room was enormous. A thick plum-colored carpet spread across the floor, its chafed surface interrupted by islands of soft furniture upholstered in grays and whites. There was a heavy Spanish table at the far end of the room, and on the wall above it was a group of small dark statues. A faint bitter odor lingered near the fireplace, its bed of mottled ashes.

"This is pleasant," I said.

"Ralph has taste." She sounded crisp, almost sharp.

I turned to look at her, but her handsome, angular face was still serene. "You're looking well," I said.

"Yes. It doesn't show."

"Show?"

"I'm pregnant, you know." She certainly was not happy about it.

"I didn't know."

Michelle started to say something, then broke off. "I'd like a drink. What can I get for you?"

"I don't drink much any more. Do you have any coffee?"

"Let's go into the kitchen. I don't know what we *do* have."

The kitchen was large enough to serve a restaurant. The stove had a console of toggle switches and signal lights, and there was a full pot of coffee on one of the coils. Michelle hesitated, flipped a switch on the stove, then began opening cupboard doors in search of a cup and saucer. She talked about the house and the hired help—a cook, a housemaid, a chauffeur-handyman—told me how awkward she felt giving instructions to people older than she was. As soon as my cup of coffee was prepared we returned to the living room.

"The kitchen makes me nervous," she said. "I'm scarcely tolerated in there until after the cook leaves. I'm supposed to write out menus and that's all. I'm not even allowed to buy groceries."

Michelle went to the sideboard and made herself a drink while I looked at the statues clustered on the wall. They were carved from wood and touched, streaked, with muddy paint. Each one was a different size but they all appeared to be rather similar in form: a lean, muscular man in a breechcloth, his legs together, his arms spread wide against the wall or stretched over his head. Some of the figures lacked an arm or a foot, and one was missing a leg. Then I saw that each one was Christ—the bodies had been taken down from their crosses and fixed to the wall.

"Poor Jesus," I muttered.

Michelle came up. "Exquisite, isn't it? Ralph says it reminds him of the Priory."

"His taste can't appeal to everyone, I suppose."

She turned from the wall and shrugged. "He makes a living at it. Everything from interiors to stage sets. It pays well."

"Where *is* Ralph?"

"He's out drinking. We used to have dinner together and then he'd go out alone to meet his friends, but we're past that now. He goes to work in the morning and I don't see him till he comes home to sleep. I suppose it sounds queer to you," she added distantly. "Actually, it's much nicer than it used to be."

We wandered down the long room to the cold fireplace. Michelle settled herself lightly on one of the divans and I sank into a deep chair across from her, trying to keep my coffee cup steady. She examined her glass this way and that, then wearily set it aside.

"Mark died," she said. "I suppose you heard."

"I knew he was dying." I stirred my coffee aimlessly, then set the spoon in the saucer.

"I heard that you quit teaching."

She was thinking of my old job at the art school. I said my lines about making more money now, and having more free time, too.

"I don't know whatever made me think I had talent. I should have gone back to France when I finished school. Oh, I was your prize pupil, all right," she said bitterly.

I felt ashamed, rotten guilty; yet we had loved each other then.

Michelle frowned, sipped her drink, then looked up. "Tell me about your new job."

I talked about my work and about Scott, told her about Marian and about Ibera. She seemed to enjoy the gossip, so I went on about Ibera and his secretaries. Close to midnight there were some small noises at a distant end of the house, then a door closed, and a few minutes later her husband appeared. I stood up.

"I thought I heard voices," he said amiably.

"You remember Frank," Michelle said to him.

Ralph and I shook hands.

"Of course. Please, please sit down. I'd like to join you but I'm really too tired to be good company. So I'm going up to bed. Stay as long as you like. Michelle doesn't often get a chance to see her old friends."

"I ought to be going soon, myself," I said.

"Please stay." He smiled, then said good night and left us.

"He seems nice enough," I ventured.

"He's plastered."

"What?"

"He's drunk, dead drunk. It took me a while to get used to it. He looks perfectly sober and he sounds all right, but tomorrow morning he won't even remember that he talked to you." She smiled thinly. "He can do all sorts of things while he's high."

It was getting on toward one in the morning when I put on my raincoat to leave. Michelle said that I must come back soon, she had few visitors; I said I would call again. We stopped each other in the Square to talk a few more times that spring, and had lunch together once, but I did not phone and she did not ask me to the house.

31

One warm Saturday afternoon in spring I took Beth's keys off the hook in my kitchen and went around to her apartment to return them. She looked blank a moment—she was in her white jersey and red shorts, same as the previous autumn—then she opened the door and stepped aside. "Come in," she said vaguely. "Meet a friend of mine." A trim young woman was seated on the sofa: her name was Milly and she worked alongside Beth at CoCo. Milly smiled politely and sat watching us.

"I came to return the keys," I said, regretting that Milly must hear me. "The car keys," I amended, lying.

Beth held them in her palm a moment, looking at them soberly, then closed her hand. "How have you been? What's new?" she asked spiritlessly.

I said that I had been well, and asked how she was.

"Oh, I'm all right." She shrugged.

"No, she isn't," Milly broke in. "She's sick. She's sick and she ought to go to a hospital, but she won't do it."

Beth looked at me—she seemed embarrassed—then walked to the cabinet and dropped the keys into the bowl. She took up a fresh pack of cigarettes, studied the seal, began picking at it with her long nails, frowning.

"What's wrong?" I asked.

"Who knows?" Beth said irritably.

"She has a cyst," Milly said. "And if you're any friend of hers you'll convince her to go to the hospital and let the doctor remove it. I've been talking to her all afternoon, but she won't listen."

"A cyst?" I said.

"On an ovary," Milly explained.

For a moment I thought I hadn't heard right. Beth seated herself heavily in one of the chairs by the table. She lit her cigarette, wearily waved the match out. She glanced at me, her face polished and blank, her eyes distant. I wanted to leave.

"That doesn't sound too serious," I said hesitantly. "It's a minor operation, I'm sure." I didn't know a damn thing about ovarian cysts.

"That's what I've been telling her," Milly said. "It's a minor operation. She'll be out of the hospital in three days."

"If it's so minor why do I have to rush right down to the hospital and get cut open? Can't I wait a while and see if it goes away? It might just go away, you know. The doctor said so himself."

"Beth, baby, you've waited long enough," Milly said. "Remember what you told me? Come on, now."

"I like me the way I am," Beth said flatly.

"You won't be any different afterward," Milly assured her. "Only healthier."

"Sure. That's easy for you to say. It's me they want to cut open. Who knows what they'll find?"

"Beth, we've been through this ten times now."

"I don't want to have any scars," Beth said sullenly.

"You'll be just as beautiful with a little scar," I told her.

"It's like having your appendix out," Milly told me. "It's not serious at all."

"Sure," Beth muttered. "I could die down here and no one would know it until the stink got too bad. Then the janitor would break in to get rid of the smell and it would be me."

"That's not true, Beth," I said.

She turned on me, her eyes glittering with anger. "Why did you bring back my keys! How will anyone get in if I'm sick!"

"We love you," Milly said. "We love you."

"What if it turns out I'm rotten inside? Will anybody love me if I can't have babies?"

"Yes," I told her. "Sure."

"Oh, Beth," Milly said. She hurried to the bowl, scooped up the keys, and crouched beside Beth, put her arm around Beth's shoulder. She rattled the keys under Beth's face. "Look. I'll take them. I'll keep them for a while. All right?"

A week later I stopped by the hospital to see Beth. She was half asleep and there was a man seated by her bed reading a magazine: his face was in the photo on Beth's bureau at home. He studied me a long moment, then gently put aside his magazine and told Beth she had a visitor. She opened her eyes. Her hair no longer glittered, but lay close upon her skull as if she had just emerged from under water. I asked her how she was feeling. "Oh, it hurts. It hurts." Her hand moved slackly across the sheets, her fingers curling at last about the man's thumb. She introduced us; his name was Bob Carter, or something, and he had flown in from Cape Canaveral. "He was here when I came out of it. And that was a good thing. They forgot to tell me about the pain." She raised Bob's hand in hers, weakly squeezing his fingers. "I've kept him here all day." She closed her eyes.

"She's so full of morphine she doesn't know what's going on," Bob said.

"Hoho," Beth said quietly, her eyes still shut. "I know what's going on. It hurts."

"You're all right, doll," he told her.

"I guess I am." She opened her eyes and looked over at me.

"You know, I told the doctor as long as he was in there he might as well take out my appendix. So he did. I have a beautiful scar now, I bet."

32

In the spring of that year I used to walk down Brattle Street—*There is a God, after all!* I thought—feeling great pity for all those people who could never have been in love as I was. One night I dreamt I was alone and with Nancy in my apartment, and it was the room I used to live in when I was a student at the Rhode Island School of Design. The room was on the second floor, front, and it had a bay window from which I used to survey a length of avenue, brick sidewalks, elm trees, large square houses: now they had torn down so many old homes that I could see the mazey plan of the streets, as if on an unfolded map of Providence. There was a light knocking at the door, and it was Alba, in her winter coat, her hair snowy and damp and her cheeks red with cold—she had run up the stairs and her eyes shone with excitement, as in the old days—"I knew you would marry her," she said, almost out of breath. She smiled cheerfully and tried to see Nancy, who was standing behind me, at my side. "Say good-by to your parents for me," she added, turning back through the doorway.

33

Today we flew kites. The students in design class have a big project toward the end of the term: each one has to design and build his own kite, then try to fly it. It's one of the traditions here. It sounds silly, but it isn't, because the students may learn something about motion and balance, and they get a chance to try out their ideas. When I took over the course I was allowed to teach it my own way so long as I ended the semester with the kites. The sun always shines on Kite Day. "Because if it rains," Hudson told me, "you just put it off for three days. It will have stopped raining by then, most likely." Hudson is chairman of the department, a tall man, gray as a birch tree. The hay field where we fly the kites has a wood at one end, and from there the land moves along flat, hops up to a little ridge, and then rolls down a long slide toward the houses in town. Nancy and I saw deer there this spring. From the road you could watch them browsing the upland meadows, setting their twig legs delicately on the sodden leaves—when you walked toward them they did not move, but if you glanced down to find your footing and then looked up, they had gone and reappeared farther away, beyond a line of red bushes, in the next pasture. Today the grass was more than ankle high and green and glossy, glistening like the coat of some mythological beast, and the breeze was strong and the sky so blue and the kites, kites up everywhere, so it was glorious.

I had roped my kite flat down on the car roof and covered the leading edge with an old blanket so it would not take off during the drive to the field. It was early in the afternoon and things were not supposed to start for a while, but when we arrived we could see a clump of people against the sky up top. I drove up the dirt ruts until they faded out, then turned the car onto the grass and parked beside Wren's motorcycle. Somebody waved to us and we waved back; then we untied the kite and started up the field—I leading as if it were a horse on a short bridle, Nancy with her hand on its flank. Wren and Thompson were there with their handiwork, and most of the others were students, too. They watched us, somewhat guardedly, as usual. "It's a great day for flying," Thompson called out, always polite. He was in a blue blazer and white yachting shoes, and his fiancée was sitting on the grass beside his kite. A couple more of my students showed up, so I got busy with them, and left Nancy talking with the fiancée, who seemed interested in pregnancies. Later Wren ambled over frowning, his dark hair down across his ears and back to the collar of his sweater. "I have a problem, big problem," he said. While I was working with him I spied Hudson's boxy wagon jouncing onto the margin of the field. A long row of cars had parked down the hill, and we were building to a good crowd—students, faculty, neighbors, children—Ruth and Dimitri turned up with their kids, and I saw Nancy talking with Sally Bush, and later with President Williams. A couple of students walked my kite a short way down the hill while I climbed back, unreeling the line until the kite bolted from their grip, shook, flapped so wildly that I thought it was going to shred, careened onto its side and slewed up again, quivering, then soared up straight, the cord burning across my hand, the kite flying up and away, far away, the line pulling hard and sagging long and heavy and firm, the kite bright, farther away now, bright gold and white.

When it was up and out as far as it could go, we drove a stake into the ground and anchored the line.

The afternoon was coming along well, I think everyone was happy, I know I felt good. Hudson had already opened one of the beer kegs, so I drew some for myself and my wife and then we strolled around to enjoy the sights. It was lovely—Nancy in her thin green gown like an unripe pear, the people walking, sitting on the hill in the warm sun, talking, the breeze bending the long grass so it shone, blowing the summer dresses, the kites that hovered above us like monstrous friendly birds, a dolphin flock. Glazer—my best student, half-cracked—had constructed a flying carousel, a merry-go-round of balsa wood and silk ribbons which rotated over our heads for a minute or two before collapsing into splinters, shreds, tatters. And Wren's kite, that gorgeous purple flower, hung upside down the whole afternoon. And Thompson had the steadiest: his was a marvelous array of blue and white boxes built into a tetrahedron, a floating pyramid. And my poor kite—I went on adding one length of string to another, fish line to twine, until some link in the anchoring cord proved too weak, snapped. It paused up there a moment, then it climbed even higher and hesitated and reared slowly over backward and headed to earth, sliding this way and that—oooh, said the crowd—trailing a wing, plunging faster until it sheared apart, dropping bits of wood, paper, wire, leaving behind only a few feathers of gold leaf which glittered and blew away. But most all the others stayed aloft, a cloud of silken tents tugging at their guy ropes. They flew all the while we talked and picnicked on the hill, all afternoon, and even later when we walked down the dampened meadow to the car we could still see two or three overhead, long creaking banners in the chill light, and the deserted field of our harmless joust.

Here in the middle of the night my mind is filled with the day, filled to the brim with daylight, and I am unable to sleep, wanting to paint. On the other edge of the campus there is a white stone chapel whose benches were removed a hundred years ago, the narrow transept and nave boxed up into classrooms, and the college has given me that chapel's second floor for my private use, a studio to work or go mad in. I spent last summer up there knocking my head against the rafters, breathing the dust of crumbling hymnals and blue books, stifling under a skylight darkened with chicken wire and bird lime, sweated, amused myself with charcoal and ink and crayon, oil paint and stone and paper and wood and canvas—I don't remember what all—made a mess. I was trying to create something that would make silence (for whenever I look at a painting, a good painting, I hear silence), but all I made was noise. Earlier this evening, after supper, we brought our coffee outside and watched Fred and Sally Bush playing badminton. Sally was working up a sweat, dashing here, there, this way, that way, slap, slap, slap—*"My point!"* she shouted. No one in the house takes the game seriously (anything is fair so long as the shuttlecock goes over the net and does not land under the chairs on one side, or in the tall grass on the other) but Sally hates to lose. She tossed the birdie into the air, whacked it sizzling over the net, began zigzagging around again. The Parovs' kids were shrieking in the house, then the screen door crashed and a moment later Dimitri Parov came padding along with a mug of coffee and a cigarette. Later Ruth Parov came out, dropped onto the cold grass, sprawled, sighing—"They're in bed. At last." And Evan Miller turned up with his mahogany lawn chair plus a couple of term papers, his face thin and pale, eyes half-lidded; he chatted languidly a bit, then began reading one of the papers. Everyone except Evan had taken a turn at playing, and now in the twilight Ruth was lobbing shots to my pregnant wife. Nancy skated back and forth to the net, heavy, bending and turning like a drenched willow tree. "It's getting late," I called to them, worried. "Why don't you quit?" But Nancy wanted to go on playing. "In a minute. In a minute," she cried. The grass was dark and the sky all faded. Evan stacked the pages neatly in his lap, shut his eyes, rubbed them, pinched the bridge of his nose. At last Nancy reluctantly quit, came over and sat down, wrapping herself in my old lumber jacket. Then we were sitting in a circle—Fred and Sally Bush, Dimitri Parov, Evan Miller, Ruth Parov, Nancy, and I—talking quietly, laughing, talking again. For two days a thousand tiny pale blue flowers had blossomed on the lawn, but now only a patch was left glowing beneath the pines—like a melting snowdrift, somebody said. No one knew what the flowers were called. The Taylors sailed over the gravel drive on shadowy bicycles, PJ's windows were lighted, and higher yet the swallows curved and dipped, twittering higher and higher into the vanishing sky. And now I cannot sleep, my mind is dizzy with the swooping flight of birds and shuttlecocks, the shaggy lawn out back, the grass that bent beneath the wind this afternoon, the heavy sag of kite strings, Nancy's watermelon belly, her green dress, and how beautiful the land is in the spring, how wonderful these friends are, how lovely my wife, how good to see the world.

34

Three days ago the bag of waters broke. Nancy was sitting in the sun on the front steps with Ruth Parov, talking while they waited for the mail—she felt it then. She stepped into the apartment for a few moments, and when she returned she said, "The baby's coming." Ruth looked at her, startled. "It's early," she said. "Six weeks," Nancy said. The mailman arrived and greeted them, began casually sorting the letters into the white boxes by the door. The women watched Ruth's kids playing on the drive, and as soon as the mailman left Ruth asked, "Did you call the doctor?" Nancy said no, not yet. "It may be a false alarm, but you should call him anyway," Ruth said. The doctor told her to stay at home, take it easy, and in a couple of days the labor pains should probably begin. Nancy told me all this when I turned up for lunch. "Good God!" I said. "I feel fine," she said brightly, sitting now at the table. "There is nothing to worry about. And there's nothing anyone can do now," she added, looking quite bland. After lunch I hung around, trying on the sly to make out if she was all right. I couldn't see any change except that she seemed distracted by my spying, so I told her I was going out to the loft to paint. But I could not concentrate. A chemical company in Cambridge had sent me a box of copolymer-base paints—acrylics of some sort—so I experimented, amused myself with them most of the afternoon, and went home early for dinner. That evening Nancy packed an overnight bag, in case she might have to go quickly to the hospital. "The last six weeks would have been dull, anyway," I reminded her. "Oh!" she said, looking up. "What are we going to name the baby?" Don't ask me why we had not yet picked a name. "Do we need one right away?" I asked. "Yes," she said. "That's the first thing they ask you when you come to your senses. Otherwise they go on calling it Baby Annunzio." I couldn't think of any names. "How about Nancy or Frank?" I suggested. We spent the rest of the evening trying to think up names. It was amazing how many names we didn't like. She favored fancy ones such as Fabrizio or Tancredi, and even a few place-names like Sicilia or Venezia (which could, she said, be cut to Vené) but after a while she said she was feeling tired, so she went to bed and we never did choose one. Nancy woke me in the dark to say that she was in labor, the pains had begun. "Are you sure?" I was still sleepy and wanted to stay in bed. "I can feel the contractions," she whispered. "And they've been coming every five minutes." I asked her if she was really sure. "I've been timing them by PJ's clock. It chimes every quarter hour. I never really listened to it before." I sat on the edge of the bed and wondered if I had time to wash and shave. "Yes. Yes. But hurry. I'm going to call the doctor," she said. The doctor told her that it would be hours before the baby arrived, but she might as well go to the hospital and wait for it there. When I had shaved and dressed I pulled up the shade in the kitchen and discovered that it was foggy outside. Nancy had made me a plate of scrambled eggs and toast; now she sat down, sipping a cup of black coffee. "Aren't you hungry?" I asked her. "I ate some toast. Please hurry," she said. "You ought to eat more. That baby is going to be doing a lot of work today." I was trying to be funny. The chapel bell was ringing for the eight o'clock class when we got into the car and started across campus. Most of the fog had burned off, leaving the air fresh and cool. "Stop at the library," Nancy cried. "I want a book and I know just where it is." I trotted into the stacks, snatched the book from the shelf, and ducked back to the car without signing the card. I asked was she ready now; she said yes, so we turned onto the highway and headed to the hospital. I was not at all as worried as I had expected, and was rather proud of myself for that. At the hospital a nurse in the lobby reported that Doctor Licht had phoned ahead of us and that he was arriving later in the morning: she led us to an elevator and we all rode to the second floor, the maternity ward. As we stepped from the elevator another nurse came forward— "Mrs Annunzio?" she asked—and led Nancy away. I hesitated in the corridor, ill at ease, abandoned, useless. A few moments later Nancy returned, held out her hands, and smiled. She looked pale and frightened. I kissed her clumsily. "Go home and get some sleep," she said. "I'm not sleepy. I'll stay here if you want me," I told her. She smiled, said no, then turned and vanished. On my way to the stairs I passed a little room with glass walls and a glass door: FATHERS. I peeped inside—two chairs, table lamp, fretted magazines—then I went downstairs and drove home.

I washed the breakfast dishes, made the bed, lit the gas under the coffee, then went to the front room to check my desk. It was the last week of the term and I had no meetings until early afternoon. The shades were still drawn and the room smelled faintly of bath powder and freshly glazed cloth. This had been my study room and now it belonged to the baby—the changing table was crated in the corner, the unpinned sides of the crib lay stacked against the wall, and Nancy had begun to fill the shelves of the rickety wardrobe with diapers, glass jars of powder, cotton balls, oil. I raised the shades and thought about assembling the crib, then went back to the kitchen and poured myself a cup of coffee. I tried to recall anyone who had had a baby six weeks early, but no one came to mind. Six weeks seemed very early to me. On the other hand, I did not know much about pregnancies and maybe it was not so uncommon as I thought. I had heard that the first baby usually came rather late. I set the empty cup in the sink and went to the front room to put the crib together; it looked easy—there were two slatted sides, a headboard and footboard, four chromium rods, and a little cloth bag with screws and miniature coil springs. I went back to the kitchen to fetch a screwdriver, then decided to have another coffee, and while I was pouring it into the cup the phone rang. It was the doctor. He said he had seen my wife, that she was in labor, was partially dilated, and that she was probably going to be in labor for a long while. "This is going to be a premature baby," he added. I said yes, I understood that, of course; I asked him how my wife was. He said that she was coming along, but that she had begun labor much too early. "This is going to be a small, premature baby, at best. We don't know how well developed or how strong it will be. We can't say much about the baby's chances for survival." I said I understood. I felt sick to my stomach. "I'm going to X-ray your wife in a little while now, to determine the position of the fetus." I asked him again how she was. He said she was cheerful, resting. He said that there was not much more that he could tell me at the moment, and that he would telephone me if there were any changes. I said thank you, and hung up, and sat at the kitchen table, tried to calm myself. The coffee was cold, bitter. I heard the Parovs' back door fly open, then tap-tap-tap as Dimitri bounced down the steps, then the crunching sound of gravel as he jogged off to class. I kept listening but couldn't hear anyone else in the house. I rinsed out the cup, then took a screwdriver from the drawer and went to the front room to put the crib together. I struggled with it for a while before I realized that it was not going to be as easy as it had looked. My fingers were stiff. I could put any two sides together but whenever I started to join a third side, then the first two would swing around half alive, flopping, screeching, slewing this way and that more wildly until the piece in hand wrenched away and the whole jumble of slats and rods slammed down in a clattering racket. My hands seemed to be frozen and the crib scared me, the way it thrashed around. I felt stupid and foolish, and was horribly afraid the baby was never coming home to sleep here. I set the sides flat on the floor, laid on the headboard and footboard, and left everything stacked by the wall. I removed my jacket and tie and stretched out on our bed for a time, then returned to the front room and untied the portfolio of sketches I had made of my wife. I looked at each one—pornographic, all of them pornographic—then tore them up, put the pieces in the fireplace, burned them. I sat at the kitchen table for a while, felt like I was shivering apart, decided to phone Sligo at his home and tell him to cancel my afternoon classes. Sligo is a decent man and has three sturdy children. He said he'd be glad to take care of it, asked me if anything was wrong. I started to tell him about Nancy, stopped, started again, began to croak, to cry. He said he'd come right over. I hung up, hot and relieved and miserable, then washed my face and put on my necktie and jacket. Sligo is a tall man with a glittering bald head, teaches art history. "Come in," I said, starting into tears. "Sorry. I don't know what's wrong with me," I added apologetically. Sligo was grave at first, and after listening for a while he suggested that we make sandwiches and have lunch. He grew cheerful later, and when we were finished eating he said, "Take it easy. You'll be all right. Let's phone the hospital." He was quite brisk. I phoned the hospital and the nurse on duty told me that there had been no change, that my wife was resting. I said thank you and hung up. "Now what?" I asked him. He looked perplexed. He shrugged and ran his hand aimlessly over his bald head. "You'll be all right," he said at the door. "Why don't you lie down and take a rest, too?"

I pulled the shades and lay on our dimmed bed and wondered how my wife was making out. When I awoke the sun was bright along the edges of the shades and the room was hot. I washed, put on my necktie and jacket, and went out to the car. Ruth was seated on the front steps with a magazine across her knees, writing a letter. She looked up, asked how Nancy was. "She's still having her baby," I told her. While we were talking Dimitri ambled out with a mug of coffee and a cigarette. He sat on the porch rail and listened, his eyes vague and evasive. "Have dinner with us," Ruth suggested. I said yes, thanks, then hopped in the car and drove to the hospital. I was the only one in that little waiting room—apparently no one else's wife was having a baby that day. Later the doctor came walking up the hall and when he saw me he smiled and strolled over. I had met Licht a couple of times before: a short man with crinkly hair and very alert eyes. Now he told me that it was going to be a breech delivery, the baby was arriving tail first, but not to worry—he foresaw no difficulties. "You look awful," he added, tapping me on the chest. "Why don't you go get something to eat?" I told him I wanted to be on hand. "You can be here by then. Nothing is going to happen until later tonight."

"I'm nervous."

"Have a drink with your dinner. Have two," he said.

I coasted down the hill and tried driving back to town slowly; the road was choked with people heading home from work, and that was all right with me. I parked on Common Street, bought a fifth of bourbon and put it in the car, then walked up to the press and got a newspaper and looked at the magazines to waste time. It seemed so strange to be idling along the half-empty sidewalk with a newspaper under my arm, in the mild sunlight just before the dinner hour, while Nancy lay in suspended labor five miles away. At last I drove back to the house, washed, took up the bottle of bourbon, and knocked at the Parovs' apartment. Ruth came to the door with shining eyes and started to embrace me. "Don't!" I croaked. "I've cried enough today." The Parovs' three kids were noisy at the table, scattering their food, climbing down from their chairs to run around the kitchen, hammering for dessert—how do they ever get born? I wondered. I drank, washed the food down with bourbon, but when the meal was over I felt as sober as before. Dimitri volunteered to drive me to the hospital. "I'm all right, my head is as clear as a block of ice," I told him. "I'll drive you anyway," he insisted. So he drove me to the hospital in his car. "The first one is the hardest," he said later. We turned up the hill in the dark, the headlights picking out the little red reflectors on the circular driveway, and when we had halted in the parking lot he asked did I want him to wait. I said no, thanks anyway: "I'll give you a call when it's over."

I sat in the empty waiting room and looked out onto the hall at the half-open doors, at the occasional visitors who arrived benign and chatty, and at a few slow women in bathrobes and floppy slippers. A short way down the hall there was a window through which you could peer into the nursery, and for a time a group had clustered there. Now only three people were left—an elegantly dressed woman with steel-blue hair, a pimpled man in a sport shirt who kept his hands deep inside his back pockets, and a girl wearing a flowered robe over her bedclothes. After the older woman had gone, the young couple pressed to the window and held a card up to the nurse beyond the glass; the nurse brought their baby and they studied it a while in silence, then moved unhurriedly down the corridor—the boy tried to walk quietly, but the iron rims on his heels tapped aloud at each step. The nurse returned to the window and, after looking out to assure herself that there were no more spectators, she shut the drapes. A heavy woman in a bathrobe came slowly up the hall with an open box of chocolates, placidly offering it to the women in each of the lighted rooms, extending it to the nurse at the desk, to me—"Have some. I can't touch them. I'll get fatter."—then she tranquilly returned to her bed, and a short time later each of the doors was shut and the overhead lights were switched off. The lamp in the waiting room remained on, but my mind was too scattered to do any reading. A short way down the hall I could see the nurse's arm writing in a pool of light at the desk, her glasses like small round mirrors, and at the edge of the corridor floor there was a tiny glowing bulb and, farther on, another and another. One of the doors which sealed off the far end of the corridor opened now and again, and this time someone was walking toward me—it was Licht. "I didn't recognize you," I said. He was dressed in loose green pajamas, operating clothes. He smiled: "Did you get your drink?" I said yes. "Good. We'll have some action for you in about twenty minutes." He paused, then added, "I've called in another doctor, a pediatrician, a very good man. He'll be with me to take the baby as soon as it's delivered. We don't expect any complications, but this is the best way. . . ." He continued to speak, told me the name of the doctor, went on saying even more, but I was unable to listen to him and heard instead simply his voice and I stared at him, trying to make out from his tone, from his mouth, his eyes, what was happening. Then he walked back down the hall, opened a door, and disappeared. *This is all make-believe*, I thought— I studied the shadowy clock above the nursery window, then hunted through the frayed magazines and finally settled on a piece about butterflies. After twenty-five minutes had passed I said the first part of the Hail Mary—*Hail Mary, full of grace, the Lord is with thee. Blessed art thou amongst women and blessed is the fruit of thy womb Jesus*—I didn't want to say the words about praying for us sinners now and at the hour of our death, so I repeated the beginning part two more times. A while later one of the doors at the far end kicked open and a doctor with a mask over his mouth hurried up the hall cradling a nest of blankets. "Are you the poppa?" he said. A ghostly yes floated out of my mouth. "You have a girl," he said, swinging past me. "It's a small one, but it's a girl." He opened the nursery door and disappeared. A nurse came up to me and asked if I was all right. I said yes. She asked if I wanted a glass of water. I said I was all right. "Let me get you some water," she said. She went off and reappeared with a paper thimble full of water; another nurse had joined us. I drank the water. One of the women lingered hesitantly while the other took the paper cup and went away. The nursery door opened slightly. The doctor told me to go to the window, then the door closed again. On the other side of the glass the doctor pulled the drapes open—the room was brightly lighted and there were tublike cribs lined against one wall—then he walked back toward the incubator: a closed glass box standing alone near the center of the room. He stood on the far side of it, jabbed his finger at the glass top to signal me, then carefully put his hands through the port holes, cupped the baby in his palms, and lifted her a bit. She looked like a bare, copper-colored bird—blind mouth, fluttering ribs, and a thick crease of flesh between her legs. The doctor lowered her gently inside the box, then withdrew his hands. He checked the lines leading to the incubator, then rolled the whole affair up to the wall and drew the curtains across my window. I went back to the waiting room and he turned up a few minutes later. "How is my wife?" I asked him. He pulled his mask down and let it dangle around his neck: "She was doing fine the last time I saw her. I'm the baby's doctor." I asked about the baby. He told me its weight, then shrugged. "I think she has a good chance, but I can't promise you anything. She could die, she's small. But she's strong and she has a chance of making it." He began to take off one of his gloves, focusing his attention on it. He peeled the rubber down his arm, inverting the glove, and his naked hand emerged pale, covered with talcum powder. "Did you tell my wife that? Does she know the baby might die?" He looked up abruptly: "I'd be a hell of a doctor if I told you one thing and her another. Wouldn't I? Of course I told her." Then a nurse came up and told me I could see my wife now. I followed her down the shadowy hall until she stopped at a half-open door, then she stood aside and I went into the lighted room.

That was three days ago, four now. We named the baby Gabriella. I never knew anyone with that name, but it seems to fit her. Nancy comes back home tomorrow while the baby will have to stay at the hospital a few weeks. I would have thought that getting born was simple. I grew up believing that life was long, love easy, and my talent as bright as an ax. I'm slow to learn. Occasionally I think I've invented the world, then after a time I come around and see that what I mistook for creation was actually my slow discovery of it. Our love for some things is so great that eventually we presume to think we own them, or even that we have created them. Yet the things of this world are not ours by our own making, but by gift, and whatever we create is ours only to delight in and let go free: only the passion is ours.

Nancy wept for a while in her room tonight, just after we had returned from viewing the baby. The baby has to stay in the isolette all the time, so Nancy never gets a chance to touch it. After the other women and the visitors have taken a turn looking through the window into the nursery, the incubator is pushed forward so that we can see it better, and we peer for as long as we like through the window, and through the glass walls at the cradle, to where she sleeps. Tonight she lay half curled, as if dreaming that she was still afloat within the womb. When we returned to the room Nancy sat in a chair by the bed and wept, cried that she wanted her child, cried bitterly. "She's my baby. I want my baby. She's mine." But even in the heat of love, even as our smallest selves, broken and incomplete, entwine like galaxies, in that moment when our joining is perfect possession, begins our dearest loss. So Gabriella uncurls like a wet fern, grows her own way.

35

There are some loose ends which need to be tied up, or at least tucked out of sight, to make this story somewhat neater. I realize that I have said very little about my paintings, but I know from experience that words are only words and that it is foolish to describe such visions. After I stopped driving all over with Beth I got together as many of my old canvases as I could stand to have in one room, painted a few more, and had a one-man show at the Zauberman Galleries in Boston. I did not do badly, so that summer Zauberman worked me into a three-way exhibit in New York where I languished for a couple of weeks and finally faded out. At the end of the summer I quit work to go on a vacation, and wound up in Provincetown, as you know. When I got back to Cambridge I looked at the unsold canvases—some of which I had hauled around for years—recognized that no one was going to take them off my hands, saw that they were dragging me down and that I would go under if I did not jettison them. That was why I chopped them up before strolling over to Research/Research one day in September. I've painted more or less steadily since then: I still do well at Zauberman's and I still get lost in New York.

As for Beth Wright: I borrowed her car once or twice that

spring to drive out to Concord, then she moved to Bob's apartment building and I never saw her again; her name was not listed in the phone book the following year, and since I did not remember Bob's last name I never learned whether she married him, or somebody else, or simply moved away.

Michelle stopped at my apartment to say good-by the night before she left for France. She was more angular, more handsome than ever, but she didn't have time to visit, so we stood just inside the door and talked about her divorce, and Michelle said, "Ralph is setting me up. He's decent in his own way." I asked how the baby was. "The baby's fine. Ralph is even afraid he might get attached to it." She laughed apologetically. Then she had to go—"I'll miss you"—and we embraced, knocking over the empty milk bottles. I have not seen or heard of Michelle since that night, but I would like to meet with her again some day and would like to learn that she is happy and that Ralph occasionally sees his son; for in spite of what she once told me, he would probably make an excellent father.

About a month after I moved out of Miss Cushing's rooming house I heard that Miss Cushing had been taken away to a nursing home; I wrote down the name of the place, because I meant to visit her, but I never got around to it and the next I heard of her she was dead.

I do not know what became of Arieh after he left the States; recently, at a cocktail party, I met an Israeli student who said he knew of an Arieh Gershom teaching at the university in Tel Aviv, and that may have been he.

Sophia Alden finally got married: Nancy and I bumped into her during the intermission of a play, and Sophia introduced her husband, a stout and rather dignified man whose name I do not remember.

Patrick Fitzpatrick passed his bar exam and joined a small law firm in Salem; he is still quite unmarried and seems to enjoy his blank private life.

It turned out that Sue Norse, the girl who told me Nancy's name, had a terror of marriage. But Nikos moved very slowly, very gently, and in time she permitted herself to succumb, to marry him, to move to the slums of New Haven where they now live while Sue works in a library and Nick teaches part-time in an art school.

Dominick Saltares knocked up Gretta Anders on one of his mad runs through Cambridge, then came back from Mexico to marry her. He had once told me to beware any woman who pleaded her belly, so now I asked him why he was so sure he was the father. "Because Gretta is disgustingly loyal," he said. "In addition, she is truthful and brave, and even if I didn't marry her she would have the baby. And any child of mine, I want to be the father."

Helen Shawn married Thomas Leverett, the man she had loved for so long, and at present they live in Switzerland. They have rented a small villa so that Leverett's daughter by his first wife can stay with them while attending a neighborhood day school, and all three move quite easily in that exotic State Department community which has grown up around the endless Geneva negotiations.

Scott has flourished. His daughter Heather married a folk singer—the only son-in-law with whom Scott gets along—and Research/Research has prospered enough to support two secretaries, the senior of whom is Marian Malone, still unmarried and more heavily made up with each passing season.

The Research/Research offices are no longer at the old address on Brattle Street. Ibera was offered a persuasive sum of money for the place by a speculator who wanted to tear down the house and put up a large brick building. Ibera in turn offered the house to the town of Cambridge for a somewhat lower price, but either the town was unable to raise the money, or they decided that the structure had no historical value apart from its age, or something. The ceilings were high, the triple-hung windows reached to the floor, there were inside shutters which folded back into reveals in the walls; it was lovely. Anyway, Ibera pulled out the marble fireplace mantels, and accepted the check from the buyer, then stood on the sidewalk in anguish while they knocked the old house flat. "He cried all the way to the bank," said Harvey Wilson. Scott now shares half of Ibera's new building, a massive two-story mansard, but it's a healthy walk from the Square.

The last time I was in Cambridge I took a walk through the Square and up and down those side streets, and I saw how much the place had changed. The old brick buildings—their iron balconies, their sandstone columns and capitals, scrolled corbels and brackets and tin acanthus leaves—most all have come down and been replaced by tall, flat cement structures. Even where the old buildings remain, the shops have changed. Max's delicatessen is gone, Cronin's has moved, Hazen's has moved, The Trap folded long ago, and a score of other coffee houses have come and gone since then, the Gabrielle—where we stopped after that cold walk by the river—is in new hands. Miss Cushing's rooming house was dumped into its own cellar and sealed over with blacktop, and all that remains is one granite step leading from the sidewalk to where the front door used to be. The small house in Spring Court where Helen and her roommates lived has been replaced by a windowless telephone building, and the courtyard itself is now paved. My Mount Auburn Street apartment vanished.

During that last visit I saw how the face of the Square had changed, and I was reminded again that it is a place for the young. It is good to have lived in Cambridge, and better yet to have been in love at the time. But it is best to move on while you can. Certain Indians believed that ghosts of the aged and the very young, too weak to make their journey to the land of shades, lingered forever about the abandoned huts where they had lived, and even at noonday you might hear the clink of pots broken long ago, or the cries of dead children driving crows from the corn. Everything changes, the world hurries on. The bridge where I took Nancy will fall some day into the river, and the water will wash over it. The Puritans who plowed their women and dreamed New England into life, the unwed Shakers who believed that the white blossoms falling in their orchard drifted ultimately to the cloudy floor of heaven, they too moved on. Only the soul will stay and not waver, for the soul is all that remains.

36

This story has no end, but let me break it off by telling you about the wedding. Mr and Mrs John Sewall White sent out the invitations to the marriage of their daughter

Anne Peregrine

to

Mr Frank Anthony Annunzio

on Saturday, the twenty-third of July, at three o'clock in the afternoon, Christ Church, Cambridge, Massachusetts. We had decided to go beyond the mere civil ceremony, had decided to get married in a church. I do not know why we chose to do this; it had never seemed important or desirable or fitting to either of us in the past. I suppose that partly we wished to mark the passage from one state of being to another, to show that this was more than one other version of the old liaisons we had untied in the past, but I think that mostly we wanted to articulate for ourselves the joining of our lives, to speak it, tell it in the language of ritual, to seize what words always fail to utter and to pronounce it at once in ceremony. Now, Nancy's parents were what they call convinced Quakers, both having been persuaded in middle age to the Society of Friends, but when Nancy was born they were still attending the Protestant Episcopal Church, so their daughter was baptized and received into that congregation. As an adolescent, under the mild influence of her parents, she took an interest in the Friends, read Fox and Woolman, and began to attend Meetings; however, nothing came of this, and during her freshman year at college she went with her Catholic roommate to Mass each Sunday throughout the spring semester and at length gave up going to any church whatsoever. When it came time to choose a place in which to get married I favored the Quaker Meeting House, but it turned out that it was no easier to join the Society of Friends than to become a Swiss citizen; on the other hand, though Nancy liked the roominess of the Catholic Church, she was eventually dissuaded by the vows and binders which her signature would lay on her as yet unborn children. So we came at last to Christ Church: a modest building designed by Peter Harrison, erected in 1759, fitted with a harmonious Palladian interior of white wood and mahogany. My parents and Nancy's parents declared themselves happy at the prospect of the marriage, and satisfied with the ecclesiastical arrangements. They had not met, but now that we were about to set the date they invited each other for tea on a couple of Sundays in June and were not alarmed, and even got along together in a fashion. The only skeptical one was Scott. "Who is this girl?" he asked me at lunch. "What do you know about her family?" I told him I was quite reconciled to the girl, that she came from an old New England family, and that her father was a school teacher, a headmaster. "You ought to investigate," he said. "There's an awful lot of nuts in New England. Some of these old families are too inbred, it makes them sickly." I laughed. He shrugged: "Well, I hope she's healthy. For your sake, I hope—" Then he broke off. He was thinking of his first wife, who had died. He flew to Europe on business a week later and when he returned he gave me a pair of ancient cuff links which he had come across in a shop over the Arno.

It was a sunny day. My brother Ed drove me to the church and all the way I tried to fight down this fear that I was going to trip, stumble, sprawl, crash when I walked to my place in front of the altar. The car rolled to a stop outside the vestry and I tore off the rented shoes—black ones with slippery leather heels—and put on the old pair which I had been carrying in my lap. In the vestry I began begging Ed to stand close beside me, closer than he had at rehearsal, to stand up against me even, then the organ changed key, the minister billowed past and gave me a tap on the shoulder, and my brother said, *All right, Frank, let's get going.* I said, *Remember not to cross yourself when he blesses us.* He said, *All right, all right, let's go.* We walked out and took our places. The groom saw his mother and father, and they both seemed pleased, contented, almost amused, and his sister Mary, who smiled and gave him the most tender glance. He turned his eyes to the door at the other end of the altar and a moment later it swung open and the bride came out—and she was beautiful—came forward on her father's arm, lifting her head to give the groom a radiant smile which he answered as best he could. Then they consented together in holy wedlock, and witnessed the same before God and that company, and thereto gave and pledged their troth, each to the other, and declared the same by giving and receiving a ring, and by joining hands; then they were pronounced Man and Wife, In the Name of the Father, and of the Son, and of the Holy Ghost.

The bride wore a ballerina-length gown of white silk faille made with a scoop neckline, three-quarter-length sleeves, and a straight front with fullness in the back. Her shoulder-length veil was of French illusion, and she carried a bouquet of white sweetheart roses and stephanotis. The maid of honor and only attendant was Miss Susanna Norse of Barrington, R.I.; Mr Edward Annunzio of Washington was his brother's best man. The ceremony was followed by a reception at the home of the bride's parents in Concord. And it was a splendid party. They had set up an open tent in back of the Whites' house, on the edge of the flat green lawn, and there our friends and relatives came to greet us and drink my uncle Cesare's champagne in the flower beds, laughing—Scott and his wife and Nancy's brother John and Marian Malone with her fiancé and Nancy's college roommate Stephanie and other of her friends I had never met before, my brother Ed and Sue Norse and my sister and Nancy's mother and Saltares and my mother and Nancy's father and her father's old uncle Peregrine who could remember before my grandfather built the big house there had been open fields where he had spent one hot afternoon haying with men who sang "Shall We Gather by the River" and Nikos and Helen Shawn (Helen came out of the sun into the yellow shade of the tent awning and said, "Ah, Frank, how did you ever pick such beautiful weather?" And her eyes suddenly glistened, overflowed, and she said, "I should have been married by now. Oh, God, Frank. I'm sorry. Is anyone coming? I'm sorry." She smiled and chatted and carefully brushed the tear away with one finger and chatted on. "We love you so much," I told her. And though it made no difference, it was true.) and Gretta Anders and Fitzpatrick and our aunts, cousins, nephews, uncles, and nieces, so many together that we were reluctant to leave. But it was time to go, time to discover how far we could sail with a few squares of canvas and a bed sheet, and so we said good-by.